LOVERS

By
J. Anderson

LOVERS

COPYRIGHT (c) 2016 JUDITH ANDERSON. ALL RIGHTS RESERVED.

No part of this book may be reproduced or transmitted in any form or by any means, electronic or mechanical, including photocopying, without permission in writing from the author.

Printed in the United States.
First Edition: 2017.

ISBN-13: 978-1977666277

Independently published by J. Anderson and loversmedia.co

This is a work of fiction. Names, characters, places, and incidents are the product of the author's imagination or are used fictitiously. Any resemblance to actual persons, living or dead, business establishments, events, or locales is entirely coincidental.

ACKNOWLEDGEMENTS

Thanks to Cindy for many years of inspiration, love, and support.

Thanks to Kate for kickstarting this novel.

Thanks to great friends Zet, El, Kyle, Marsha, Eve, Mariah, Gloria, Alice, Canfield, Laura, Patty, Sabra, Mitzi, Rebecca, Chip, Kate, Nancy, and Gerry, who all shared much love and good times.

Ditto my family—you are the best!

Wherever you have friends, that's your country
and wherever you receive love, that's your home.
Dalai Lama

- 1 -

A long, lean, yellow tiger cat sauntered down the driveway toward the guesthouse, ignoring the huge German shepherd hurtling toward him at a full run. About a foot from the cat, the dog turned—too late to avoid slamming into the chain-link fence between them. The cat sat down, elegantly raised a back leg, and began an unnecessary bath. On the other side of the fence, the dog went crazy, gnashing its teeth against metal, then alternating frantic digging with attack-barking.

The ruckus finally reached Kyle Chandler's awareness. Still in boxers and undershirt, she sat on the living room floor of the guesthouse, surrounded by jeans, shirts, music gear, hiking gear, backpack, books, files—basically everything she owned—plus an open suitcase and random boxes. Supposedly packing, she found herself staring at an old photo when the noise got to her.

Irritated, she yelled toward the open window, "RAT! GET

IN HERE. NOW!"

Outside, the barking abruptly turned to whining. Then silence. In moments, the cat jumped onto the windowsill and, in one leap, landed gracefully in Kyle's open suitcase. Innocently, he circled Kyle's best shirts, flopped down, and began to purr.

"You are totally ridiculous, Rat," said Kyle affectionately.

With half-closed eyes, Rat stared back at Kyle without seeing or hearing, drifting into meditation on chaos and change.

"Alright, where was I?" Kyle felt the photo she still held in her hand, one she had printed but never framed.

In the haze of a lesbian bar, five scruffy women with foolish grins and their arms around each other, looked out at her, laughing. Unconsciously, she smiled back. Her band, *DQ.* Short for *Drama Queen, Dirty Queer, Dyke Quotient,* and countless other forgotten names. Furrowing her brow, Kyle studied the woman in the middle—radiantly physical, spiky hair, loose shirt and jeans, totally *there* without apology, and oh, so young—herself three years ago.

She picked up another photo out of the old shoebox in front of her and laughed out loud. *DQ on-stage. Nandi out front, singing. Or crying. Or having a multiple orgasm. Or everything at once.* Nandi Johnson. Kyle's best friend. Totally unique goddess of sound. Heart of gold. Clueless about her own power. Kyle smiled warmly and turned to the next photo.

Jessie! Kyle's stomach clutched involuntarily. *Jessie with Kyle. Close up, intimate.* Jessie looking with love at the camera, looking like an incarnation of love. Kyle entranced, light-hearted, invincible. Beautiful together. Archetype lesbian lovers. Born for each other.

"Fuck! Fuck! FUCK!" Kyle ripped the photo in two, then four. Furious, she flung the pieces in the direction of the trash.

- 2 -

In the main house, Nandi and her roommate, Kay, lingered over a cup of coffee at the kitchen table. Talking quietly, they watched Kyle loading her pickup in the driveway. They should be out there too, loading Nandi's stuff. But Nandi could not pack. She needed just one more minute of this timeless here-and-now. Maybe two more minutes. Tomorrow, she and Kyle would be on the highway to Tucson. *Shit.*

Nandi hadn't seen or talked to her on-again-off-again lover, Jackie, for three months. And two and a half days. She still loved Jackie. But she was being strong. Or so her friends said. Whatever. For better or worse, this time it was a clean break. Jackie usually exploded at Nandi, walked out, and crawled back within a week. This time, for the first time, Nandi felt it coming and watched it happen, as if someone else was going through the motions. And for the first time she was tired of the whole mess. In the emptiness of the past months, her friends redoubled their advice to get tough, get free, and get over it.

Lovers

And just when she was sure it was done, Jackie offered a half-assed apology. She never replied, knowing the breakup was overdue. Her friends were ecstatic. Supportive. Hopeful for her. A summer get-away with Kyle would be perfect. They would return home transformed by a great adventure.

But the perfect idea became a nasty reality as soon as Nandi tried to pack. Fear poured in to fill the deep, silent void Jackie left in her heart. Thanks to Jackie, she doubted her ability to do anything, be anything, alone. Kyle was the last person she could confide in, because Kyle had hated Jackie from the beginning. Kyle kept saying that a summer of love was waiting in Tucson. Of course, Kyle didn't believe it either, but she was at least going through the motions. Kyle never really looked forward to anything after Jessie left. How could she? She was determined to feel nothing except *How are you? Fine. Let's go to bed.* Nandi hated her own void, although hers was deeply lonely, not filled with meaningless one nighters and affairs.

So Nandi poured her heart out to Kay.

What if Nandi hated Tucson? What if she couldn't find a job? What if she couldn't make friends? Nandi went on and on, unable to face her empty suitcases. Her worst, unspoken fear lurked beneath the conversation like a black widow weaving an elaborate web under the table. Tomorrow, a new roommate would take Nandi's room for the summer. Kay had arranged it. A financial necessity. A burned bridge. And now the only real issue was: *What if Nandi wanted to come back? What if she really couldn't live without Jackie?*

"Oh, crap. Here comes trouble."

Through the window, they watched Kyle stomp across the yard toward the back door. Nandi's huge German shepherd, Michelle, dogged her heels, wagging. Sweaty and pumped up

5

with annoyance, Kyle threw open the door and slammed it behind her, consciously cutting off Michelle. She broke into her friends' intimacy like a baseball through a glass window. Feeling the shock caused by her entrance, she stopped short, losing her momentum.

"Hey, Kyle," said Kay, ever mellow, offering her a chair. "Have some coffee. We've been watching you load the truck."

"Well, thanks, Kay. I really appreciate that!" Kyle remained standing. "You guys ready to load Nandi's stuff?"

"Well, uh..." said Nandi, searching for a palatable approximation of truth. "I'm still packing."

"Well of course you are. I can see that."

Tweaked, Kyle went to the cupboard for a mug. Guilt-induced smiles flashed across the table between Nandi and Kay. Resigned, Kyle sat down and Kay poured her some coffee. There was an awkward silence. Kyle shot Nandi a hard look across the table.

"Guess I'd better pack." Nandi pretended to hurry to her room.

"She's having a hard time," said Kay, when Nandi was out of earshot.

"I know. I know." Kyle shook her head, and then unexpectedly confided, "I don't blame her, Kay. This trip is idiotic."

"Jesus, Kyle, not you too."

"Well, what was I thinking? Spending the *summer,* for God's sake, in Tucson, Hundred and Ten Degrees, Arizona!"

"Well, I still think swapping houses with Liz for the summer is a great idea," Kay said unconvincingly.

"Yeah," Kyle challenged, "But would *you* do it? No!"

"No, but..."

"Let's face it—we're talking summer in the fuckin' desert! Two zombies in hell…"

Kay laughed and gave up.

"I mean why didn't Liz just rent a house for the summer," Kyle went on. "We would've all had a blast. But *no*...It had to be a house swap."

Kay asked, "Why *are* you doing it, Kyle?"

"I don't know—I had a feeling when Liz asked me...

Kay almost said *follow your bliss*, but stifled it. Kyle would have killed her with a look of death.

"And now?"

Kyle admitted, "It's weird. It still feels right—*and* idiotic!"

Kyle laughed and shifted back into gear. "Thanks for the coffee. I'll go *really* clean my house this time."

Heading out, she yelled down the hall, "NANDI! Get your butt in gear. Don't make me come in there..."

There was no funny answer from Nandi's room. No answer at all. Kyle didn't push it. There was no way she was going to initiate a talk. She knew Nandi would back out at the slightest, most microscopic, opportunity...

- 3 -

Just past midnight. The rainbow neon over San Diego's lesbian bar bounced off of all the glass and chrome in sight. A tall, charismatic, young black woman approached the bar alone. Nandi's ex, Jackie, felt her body resonate with the heavy beat of the drums and bass oozing from the bar. Wearing eight hundred dollars worth of clothes on a toned body, she exuded sex and power, a highly magnetic combination for the unwary.

Two skinny leather girls smoked outside the door to the bar. One, with her knee bent and her foot against the building, stared at Jackie, craving her attention. The beckoning length of white, tattooed leg and pierced smile went unnoticed as Jackie brushed past the women and opened the door. A tidal wave of sound and frenetic energy assaulted her.

Jackie entered the sea of women's bodies. Instinctively, the crowd parted to let her in. The thunderous heartbeat of the band animated the crowd as one sensuous being—dancing, kissing, flirting, fighting, shouting bits of conversation, falling in and out of love and lust. Above it all, ruling it all, Nandi's deep goddess voice. Then Kyle's rough harmony, a beautiful match. Jackie knew the tune, the band's signature song that Kyle had written long ago. In fact, Jackie knew everything that would follow. The song, the words, the thrill of moving toward Nandi through the crowd, the women parting to let her pass, following her with their eyes. And, finally, Nandi's unguarded look of adoration as she looked down from the stage to find Jackie approaching her.

But, this time Nandi caught herself quickly and looked away. Not missing a beat, she grabbed the mic off the stand and jumped into the crowd. With a circle of fans around her, she sang the last chorus of the very last song to a cute little dyke. She was all over the woman, brazen, hot and sexy. The crowd loved it. There was wild cheering when the song ended.

"Thank you! We love you. That's it," Nandi said. She jumped back on-stage and did a silly, elaborate rapper handshake with Kyle.

The crowd began to chant, "More! More!"

Plaintively, Nandi sang, "Yeah it's gonna be...

Kyle harmonized, "...a long, lonely summer."

Lou, the shortish, plumpish bar owner, ran on-stage carrying two huge gift-wrapped boxes. She juggled them as she took Kyle's mic and waited for the crowd to settle down.

"Alright. Alright. Nandi and Kyle, we'll miss you. As a, uh, small token of our appreciation..."

"Yeah, right..." Nandi said, expecting a practical joke. "Rubber chicken? Tickets to Barry Manilow?"

"What?" said Lou, defensive. "Seriously, Nandi. As I was saying...Oh, hell. Here. Take it."

Tentatively, Nandi unwrapped a very expensive turquoise

cowboy hat with a beautiful, beaded band. "Whoa!"

Someone in the crowd yelled, "Put it on! Put it on!"

Nandi took off her African cap and modeled the Stetson. Although it fit perfectly, it was instant culture clash with her close-cropped hair, piercings, beads, and earrings.

Vamping it up, Nandi looked over her shoulder seductively, "Am I not the perfect cowgirl?"

Several women yelled, "Take it off! Take it off!"

Nandi drew imaginary pistols and shot the loudmouths in the crowd. *DQ*'s drummer supplied sound effects. The victims fell to the floor, and friends dragged them back to their feet.

While they waited, Kyle whispered something in Lou's ear and they laughed privately. Lou blushed. Her longtime crush on Kyle was obvious. Lou passed the other present to Kyle, "This one's for you, Kyle. Have a blast. But don't forget *this* is home."

Like a little kid, Kyle unwrapped a pair of sleek, black western boots. She held them up for the crowd's *oohs* and *aahs*. Kyle hugged Lou sincerely, then took Nandi's mic and turned to the crowd, "Thanks, Lou. Thanks everybody! We love you!"

There was nothing else to say.

Always no nonsense, Lou concluded, "That's all, women. Thanks again for coming. And now the bar's *closed*."

The crowd dispersed slowly. Supremely aware of Jackie's presence, Nandi focused instead on friends and fans that came to the stage to say goodbye. She smiled and hugged and spoke without breathing or feeling or hearing, and tried to ignore the ecstasy and fear pounding in her heart. Kyle, too, was surrounded by women, but oblivious to Jackie and the change in Nandi.

In a private corner, under the TUCSON OR BUST sign, Kay and her friend Denise pulled a couple of tables together, then sat down to wait for the good-bye toast planned for a few close friends.

Kay said fondly, "Look at Nandi in that 50-gallon hat. And that heartbreaker, Kyle."

"Even I slept with her, remember? Right after Jessie ditched her," Denise said, cynically. "Kyle apologized twice the next day. The old *let's not ruin our friendship* thing."

"Good line..." Kay replied.

Suddenly, Kay's stomach clutched as Jackie came suddenly into focus in the background, waiting for Nandi like a snake in tall grass.

"Goddammit! Dracula! What the hell is she doing here?" Kay exploded and bolted from the table, heading for Jackie.

"Kay, wait!" Denise ran after her.

Stopping short, right in Jackie's face, Kay snarled, "Get out, Jackie. Leave Nandi alone."

"Lose it, Bitch!" Jackie snapped, and then looked past her.

Seeing trouble, Lou bellowed, "Closing time! *Goodnight, Kay. Goodnight,* Jackie."

"Jackie??!!" Kyle blurted out, "NO, dammit! Let's get outa..."

But Nandi was already gone, heeding the call of drama. She ran to the confrontation where Kay was spewing every nasty word she knew. Nandi wedged herself between them both, as Kyle arrived, right on her heels. Everyone fell dangerously silent.

Nandi addressed Jackie with surprising calm, "S'up, Homegirl?"

"I need to talk to you."

"It's over. We've talked it to death."
Yeah! Be strong! Kyle thought.
"Things have changed," said Jackie.
Kay broke in, "Nandi, come *ON*."
Jackie ignored her. "Nandi, it's been so long. Please come and talk."
It was the seemingly heartfelt *please* that got her. Nandi took off the cowboy hat and handed it to Kyle, not daring to meet Kyle's gaze.
"Fifteen minutes, outside," Nandi told Jackie, dispassionately.
"NO!" Kay groaned.
"No. Nan..." said Kyle, refusing to take the hat.
Nandi insisted, meeting Kyle's eyes with surprisingly strong resolve. "Get me at nine-thirty, Kyle. Just like we said. I'll be ready."
"Don't do this, Nan," Kyle implored.
"No shit. No worries. I'm going with you no matter what."
Kyle shook her head.
"*I promise.*"
Kyle took the hat. Nandi left with Jackie. Her friends watched in disbelief as the door closed shut behind them.

-4-

Later, in the empty bar, Lou poured tequila shots for Kyle, the band and a few close friends. The table buzzed with speculation. Kyle leaned back in her chair, staring at the table—silent, defeated, and totally in shock.

"You think she'll go back with Jackie?"

"Duh. She already did, didn't she?"

"I can't believe Jackie showed up," Lou grumbled,

"She's right on schedule. That's what pisses me off," growled Kyle.

Kay took the reins, lifting her glass, "C'mon, let's send Nandi some love, however dumbshit she's being right now."

Everyone toasted, "To Nandi!"

Lou poured another round.

"Okay, Kyle," said Denise, "Kay said your friend, Liz, is coming for the summer. What's the deal?"

"We're doing a summer house swap. She's in grad school at U of A in Tucson, doing a summer project at UCSD," Kyle explained.

Denise said, "Cool, but is she cute? Is she single?"

Kyle smiled. "Yeah, very cute. And very single, at least as of yesterday."

Denise lit up, "Alright! To Liz!"

Pouring again, Lou said, "Okay, this toast is for Kyle..."

Kay interrupted, "Kyle, you slut, it just hit me. They're probably talking about *you* right now at some bar in Tucson..."

Lou interrupted, "Can't we get to the toast? I did not say *roast*."

Kay, pretending seriousness, raised her glass. "To Kyle Chandler. Temp talent for Tucson!"

Denise took the bait, "Diva for the desert..."

Cutting them off, Lou broke in, "How about this: To Kyle, new grrl in town. Have an awesome adventure and come back soon!"

As the women raised their glasses, Kyle added, "Nandi too. New *grrls* in town."

Denise mumbled, "Don't hold your breath."

Everyone else went along and happily toasted, "New grrls in town!"

Meanwhile, back home, Nandi and Jackie were having the best goodbye sex of their lives.

- 5 -

Kyle awoke in a panic. The alarm, set maximally loud, was jackhammering into her monstrous hangover headache. Naturally, she pounded the fucking thing to death. *Oh, for god's sake.* Denise was by her side, shirtless, turning over to go back to sleep. *How could I bring somebody home last night? And how can Denise be that stupid?* Without rousing the woman, she got up and lunged toward the bathroom with the walls spinning around her. She was still royally drunk.

Ready for death, Kyle downed four ibuprofen. Before the pills could work, she puked them up and felt slightly better. She took more ibuprofen with sixty gallons of water.

Staring into the mirror, disgusted, the whole travesty of last night suddenly came back to her. *Nandi, dammit!*

Kyle pulled on her traveling clothes, buttoning her shirt one buttonhole off, which, incidentally, nobody dared to tell her about all day. She worked on her challenged hair. Even when she put on a cap, some of it still stuck out behind her ears.

She woke Denise. Aware of Kyle's foul mood, Denise left immediately, in disarray, kissing Kyle's cheek on the way out—all she was offered. Kyle mumbled goodbye.

Almost throwing up again, Kyle opened a can of wet food for Rat, who had wisely remained scarce until exactly that moment. While Rat ate, Kyle cleaned up the last remnants of her life, and made up the futon. She was glad she did the major cleanup yesterday. Her killer headache drowned out any other thoughts or feelings. It was already nine and she was desperate for coffee.

Kyle dragged herself up the back steps of the main house. *Goddammit!* The door was still locked. Frustrated beyond words, Kyle knocked loudly. On the flip side of the door, Michelle did her watchdog routine, designed to scare the crap out of any living thing. Pausing not at all, Kyle knocked harder, then banged on the door. She withheld any consoling words for Michelle, letting the dog go completely crazy to wake everyone up inside.

"Geez, Kyle." Kay finally opened the door, still half asleep. Recognizing Kyle, Michelle raced outside to take care of more important things.

"Sorry." Kyle immediately felt a big wave of compassion for Kay, who looked exactly like Kyle's own hangover would look if it were a dyke.

"Where's Nandi?" Kyle knew it was bad news to have to ask.

"Dracula's here," said Kay, shaking her head. She gestured down the hall to Nandi's closed bedroom door.

"Shit!" Kyle went over the top. She stomped down the hall and knocked hard on Nandi's door. "Nandi! Are you there? NANDI!" Kyle knocked again. "Are you coming??"

"Okay. OKAY! Okay."

Nandi emerged half-dressed from her room. Her eyes were puffy and nearly shut. She had probably just gotten to sleep. She smelled like sex.

"Hi..." she said in a gravel voice. She quickly closed the door behind her, but Kyle got a glimpse of Jackie, pretending to be asleep in Nandi's bed.

"*Hi???* Get a grip, Nan! What the hell are you doing? Are you coming or not?"

Nandi offered, "Yes, I'm coming. Okay? I'm sorry, okay? You woke me up, okay?"

She headed for the kitchen with Kyle dogging her heels. Nandi put up her hand "no"—as in no more discussion—and Kyle relaxed a little. Kay was putting on some water to boil. Still groggy, Nandi fumbled with the coffee jar. Eight hundred coffee beans flew across the counter in slow motion.

"Uh-huh," she said, so very quietly, ready to explode. She scooped up some beans into the grinder.

"You don't *have* to come, you know."

"Dammit, I'm coming, Kyle. Can't you have a heart, for once? It's our last good-bye." Nandi pressed the grinder top repeatedly. Nothing happened.

"Last good-bye?" Kyle launched into a diatribe as Nandi fooled with the grinder and Kay quietly plugged it in.

BZZZAAAATTT! Nandi ran it forever, cutting Kyle off. Not to mention sawing through three layers of Kyle's headache.

"Okay, our fucking bazillionth last good-bye," Nandi admitted. "Now, make the goddam coffee and I'll be ready in a minute. I have to pack."

Much later, sitting on the back steps, Kay and Kyle finished their third cup of coffee. Kyle's foot jiggled continuously to burn off the energy. Periodically, Nandi came to the door with a box or suitcase, which they quickly packed.

Finally it was time. Kyle went to the guesthouse and wrote a welcome note for Liz. She looked around one more time, feeling as nostalgic as her headache allowed. For a moment, tears welled up in her eyes. She was grateful for her simple home.

"C'mon, Ratty," Kyle called sweetly, getting the cat carrier.

Rat didn't come.

"Rat?" a little louder, a little firmer.

No Rat. Nowhere in sight.

A moment later, Kyle added forcefully, "Rat, don't pull any shit on me now."

Rat came immediately. He was the smartest cat in the world.

As soon as Kyle closed the carrier door, Rat began to howl. Both Kyle and Rat accepted this as a given. Kyle grabbed the carrier, put Rat in the back seat, and waited at the truck. Kay came over, and both dykes leaned against the truck, waiting. And waiting. Rat howled more quietly now, with an occasional whine thrown in. At one point, Kyle and Kay exchanged glances, rolled their eyes, and burst out laughing. Kyle lay down in the grass and closed her eyes. Kay threw the ball a few godzillion times for Michelle.

Finally, Nandi and Jackie emerged and briefly, thank god, kissed goodbye. Nandi called Michelle and got her onto the leash.

Lovers

"No, Michelle. Heel! Come on! No!" Nandi said, yanking the muscular dog, who pulled enthusiastically in the opposite direction.

"Take care, Buddy," said Kyle, "Come visit."

Hugging her roughly, Kay said, "Love you, Kyle. Safe trip."

Meanwhile, Nandi and the dog zigzagged toward the truck. Michelle was not fond of rides, which she associated with going to the vet. Jackie draped herself over the porch railing, showing ample cleavage, and called to Nandi, "Beautiful night, wasn't it? We're not finished yet."

Kyle revved the engine to drown her out. Kay held her tongue and held open the passenger door. At last, Michelle bounded onto the seat. Tears running down her cheeks, Kay gave Nandi a big hug goodbye. Then, looking longingly backward, Nandi called a simple goodbye to Jackie. She climbed heavily into the truck, as if lifting the weight of the world. The sound of Kay closing the door was the happiest sound Kyle had ever heard.

Jackie yelled, "Call me from the highway," and blew Nandi a kiss.

Kyle backed out of the driveway at maximum speed, throwing Michelle onto Nandi's lap. Rat howled in the back seat. Michelle responded by lunging over the seat toward the carrier. The little trapped Rat hissed through the bars, eyes wide with fear. Michelle barked frantically. Holding the dog back with all her strength, Nandi yelled, "Sit! Michelle! SIT!"

With Kay and Jackie becoming ever smaller in the rear view mirror, the whole dog-and-cat circus distracted Nandi from a full theatrical goodbye. Finally, Kyle stopped, grabbed Michelle's collar, looked directly into the dog's wild eyes, and commanded, "NO!"

The dog froze. Very cold and quiet, Kyle commanded, "NO—or you're dogmeat."

Michelle immediately sat down and panted happily.

"*Dogmeat?*" Nandi said.

They both laughed hysterically until tears ran down their faces. All tension between them evaporated. At the highway, Kyle floored the engine and got reacquainted with her headache. Nandi cried non-stop for an hour.

- 6 -

They left San Diego some time after noon. By one, Nandi had cried through every Kleenex in the glove compartment. Finally, she confessed, "Jackie wants me to move in with her."
"Of course. She tells you now that you're leaving—er, left."
"I still love her, Kyle."
"God knows why."
"She's good in bed."
They both laughed. But, it was a simple truth any fool could understand. Beyond that, it had become very complicated.
Exhausted, Nandi leaned her head back on the seat and closed her eyes in total surrender. She heaved a big sigh and drifted into a nap. Michelle nudged close. Rat already slept peacefully in back.
Blessed silence! A miracle must have occurred!

For a long time, Kyle drove and Nandi slept. The heavy wind and the straining engine blended into a weird roar. Kyle pushed them forward, well over the speed limit, trying to put a million miles between them and Jackie.

-7-

Kyle looked over tenderly when Nandi stirred, her hard concentration softening into a smile. "Hi, Girlfriend!"

Looking outside, Nandi exclaimed, "What? Where are we? Mars or Egypt?"

"Imperial Dunes. Biggest in North America."

"Unbelievable!"

Massive sand dunes, dotted with ATVs and motorbikes, spread along the highway as far as they could see. Kyle pulled off at the Gordons Well exit and headed for a pit stop at Duner's Diner, a tiny hole in the wall dwarfed by the dunes.

While Nandi walked Michelle, Kyle pumped gas and got them some coffee and snacks to go. She took Rat outside in her little harness, which Rat considered extreme maltreatment. Kyle offered the cat some water and dry catfood, which Rat ignored. Ditto the perfect, golden sand that was the essence of this landscape. Only Rat could decline the biggest cat box in the world! Finally, Kyle returned the offended cat to the carrier. Rat immediately closed his eyes to dream better dreams than the current reality could offer.

Leaning against the truck, Kyle looked after Nandi, who had walked Michelle—or vice versa—quite far down the service road. Nandi had taken out her cell as soon as she was out of earshot. As she returned from the distance, Kyle could see that she was intensely absorbed in conversation, to whatever extent possible while yanking Michelle out of the scrubby bushes at the side of the road.

Back on the highway, no one talked about the phone call. Don't ask; don't tell. Kyle knew that any shot at Jackie would send Nandi rushing to her defense. They cranked the music and sang along. Nandi texted while Kyle drove on, past Yuma and into the desert wilderness.

After another two hours on the road, they were lured by a giant billboard plate of fried chicken. Following its call, they pulled off the highway and ordered dinner at a not so famous roadside cafe. Nandi "forgot something outside" and left to call Jackie. But, what she actually forgot was to charge her cell phone overnight. Within minutes, she blew back in. When Kyle refused to lend her her phone, Nandi angrily found the pay phone, and started a long and expensive collect call.

Kyle texted Liz and Kay and then stared out the window into the middle of nowhere. Road-tired and disoriented, she looked past her pickup and the one lone car out front to watch the highway beyond. It was truly a "ribbon of a highway" across a desolate landscape of scrub brush and dirt. Above, beautiful fluffy clouds crept across the big, big sky, including

Lovers

some giants that could cloak an alien mother ship with no problem. Except why would aliens have any interest in this place? Inside, there was the lingering smell of burgers, stale oil and Nandi's disgusting, untouched, chicken dinner across the table. Kyle's had already been delivered, half-eaten, and the greasy plate taken away.

Nandi gestured emphatically in the phone booth. The only other customer, an elderly man in polyester, paced outside, waited for a few minutes, then returned to his table.

"Dammit, I forgot to charge it," he said loudly to his wife. Then, the couple both laughed! Kyle was happy for them. No blame was hurled. No dirty looks or silent treatment like there would have been in Kyle's own family. Still, Kyle had to smile at God's sense of humor. The fact that the only other people in this god-forsaken place needed the pay phone too, at this exact moment in time, was too cruel to be a coincidence.

After some time, the man went back to wait at the phone booth. How much longer could it be? At last, Nandi threw the door open and ran out, letting the receiver drop on its cord.

The man muttered, "You gotta be kidding..."

"One more minute..."

Nandi crash-landed across from Kyle. "Wanna go back?"

"Get real, Girlfriend." Kyle had to look away. She was really pissed!

The man yelled, "HEY! Are you still on?"

"Listen to this. You go back to the guesthouse. We lose the new roommate. Liz takes my old room. And I'll stay with Jackie."

"Whatever you just said, no way! I'm not going back."

Waving the receiver, the man yelled, "I'm hangin' this up now..."

Nandi looked frantically at Kyle.

"No way!"

Nandi ran and grabbed the phone, slamming the phone booth door behind her.

"Come *ON!*" The nice man finally lost it and pounded the hell out of the door until Nandi hung up.

Nandi apologized, then sheepishly sat down across from Kyle and pushed her food aside. Kyle looked at her and said nothing. Clearing her throat, Nandi admitted, "I'm going back. Jackie's gonna get me."

Kyle slumped back in her chair. "Goddammit. Get you where?"

"Here."

"I can't believe it."

"What?" said Nandi, reading her mind. "You don't have to wait."

"I can't leave you here. What if she doesn't come?" That was a low blow and Kyle knew it. Unfortunately, it was also a very real possibility, based on past experience.

"Kyle, you are a real asshole."

"Right. *I'm* the asshole."

"Kyle, I'm sorry. Try to understand..."

Kyle was out of patience. "Okay, why'd she show up last night, not a week ago?"

"It finally hit her that I was leaving. She's changed. I can hear it in her voice."

Kyle was furious beyond words. She had to look out the window or explode.

Nandi pressed on. "Jackie finally realized she loves me, you idiot. Please be glad. We're gonna move in together."

"Good luck," Kyle groaned cynically, unable to swallow

Nandi's self-destruction another second. She leapt to her feet at the exact moment the waitress arrived at the table with a fresh pot of coffee. When they collided, the glass carafe crashed to the floor.

Kyle mumbled, "Sorry," as she stormed outside, crushing shards of glass underfoot as she escaped.

Later, Nandi apologized, ordered a new dinner, and finally ate. Having nothing left to say, the two friends watched the broken stream of headlights and taillights on the highway. Every so often they went outside. They gave Rat and Michelle their dinners, and then took Michelle on a long walk along the deserted service road that led to the remote cafe. The sky had filled up with more stars than either of them had ever seen. Hanging motionless over the cafe, the almost-full moon bathed the brilliant blue emptiness with a silver haze. It was eerily quiet, except for the occasional trucks on the highway.

"Nan?" Kyle eased into a difficult subject. "I'm gonna miss you."

Nandi's eyes welled up with tears.

"Don't take any shit this time, promise me."

Nandi started to cry, put up her hand for Kyle to stop.

Kyle continued, gently. "Listen, if it doesn't work out, please come to Tucson. Okay? Any time, day or night. I want you to come."

Nandi's eyes teared as she took in her best friend's love and forgiveness. "You're the best, Kyle."

"You too, Nan. I'm serious. She should...love you back."

Nandi put her arms around Kyle and cried like a baby. Kyle held her. Michelle sat down on Nandi's shoe and leaned against her leg. Later, they put Michelle back in the truck, where Rat was already in his crate, snoozing. A bottomless cup of coffee, phone surfing, and two magazines later, the glare of Jackie's headlights momentarily blinded Nandi and Kyle.

"There she *IS*!" yelled Nandi, leaping up in ecstasy. With the abandon of true love, she raced out to embrace Jackie. Jackie kissed Nandi quickly, and then went directly inside to use the restroom and get something to eat. She ignored Kyle completely and was mercifully ignored in return.

Kyle helped Nandi load her stuff into Jackie's car. The last box was Nandi's Stetson hat, but Nandi asked Kyle to keep it. With the transfer done, Kyle and Nandi looked at each other and laughed at the absurdity of it all. It was that or cry. Kyle moved Rat's carrier to the front seat, hugged Nandi goodbye, jumped in, and fired up the truck. She couldn't linger in this unwanted reality another minute or she would say or do something she'd regret.

As the truck pulled away, Nandi yelled, "You go grrl. I love you!"

Dwarfed by the lonely landscape, Nandi and Michelle watched the red lights of Kyle's truck enter the highway and disappear into the starry night.

-8-

Exhausted and bedraggled, Kyle knocked on Liz' front door some time after midnight.

"Kylie!" Liz screamed happily, and the two women hugged like the long-lost friends they were. Rat howled in his carrier on the welcome mat.

"C'mon in," Liz grabbed Rat's carrier and Kyle's traveling bag.

Kyle got her keyboard and Rat's catbox and food from the truck, then followed Liz inside. The little brick house was like a cabin mated with a greenhouse. There were beamed ceilings, red wood paneling, simple furniture and plants everywhere. Kyle instantly loved it.

"Home sweet home," Liz gestured widely.

"It's great," said Kyle, totally devoid of energy. Liz was worried. Kyle looked terrible. She was never this...blank.

"What exactly happened to Nandi?" Kyle had called and texted several times from the road, but Liz could make no sense of it other than Jackie took her back to San Diego.

"The usual, but worse. Tell you later. I'm beat."

Liz asked, "Are you hungry? Want a beer?"

"No, thanks. I need to crash." Kyle opened the door to the cat carrier. "C'mon out, Ratty. This is it."

Rat balked, looking around, paranoid.

"C'mon, little Rat," Kyle coaxed.

"Aw, he's scared," said Liz. "I'll take care of him after you're settled."

Liz led Kyle through an obstacle course of stuff in the hallway. At the second bedroom, Liz said, "Take this for now. Bathroom's right there. Um, I'm having a little party tomorrow. Hello-goodbye thing. Hope that's alright..."

"Great. I just need a little sleep."

"Sweet dreams, Girlfriend." Liz shut the door behind her.

Kyle peeled off her clothes and fell into bed. In ten hours, she awoke in a new world, showered, and rejoined the human race.

-9-

Liz and Kyle worked together easily in the kitchen, cutting vegetables into a huge salad for the potluck. Some of Liz' closest friends were already hanging out in the living room.

The doorbell rang, and the next moment the most striking couple Kyle had ever seen appeared in the kitchen. Allie, a stocky, self-confident African-American woman, preceded her gorgeous Latina lover, Christina. Each carried a bottle of wine, which they passed on to a woman who seemed to be getting everyone drinks.

As they chatted and got a glass of wine, Kyle leaned over to Liz, "God. Great couple."

Allie was charismatic, a natural leader. Kyle was struck by her vital energy, her *presence*. In contrast, Christina was taller, subtle and fine, every detail fascinating.

"Yeah, together six years. Allie's my best friend here—teaches high school biology, coaches softball, mentors the youth group. Christina's a nurse, does Reiki…"

As Liz described her friends, Kyle noticed Christina's long fingers around the neck of the wine bottle. Two simple rings. Her gaze moved to the two-button length of sky-blue shirt open at Christina's neck, the perfect skin and close-fitting, delicate gold chain.

"Hey, Liz-beth!" Allie came in first.

"Hey, you guys. Allie, this is Kyle."

Extending her hand warmly, Allie said, "Hi. This is my partner, Christina."

Partner. Fair enough, thought Kyle. *I can see that you're part of each other, more than any word could express.* "Good to meet you both," she said out loud, shaking Christina's hand.

"Yeah, welcome to Tucson," Christina said. Then, putting her arm around Liz's shoulder, she added, "We're gonna miss this one, though."

Allie said, "Are you excited, Liz?"

"Ah, kind of in shock. You know what I mean, Kyle."

Kyle grabbed at the air with her hands and did a great impromptu freak-out, complete with an anguished, "AAGH!"

"YAAHH!" Liz added a slightly stifled scream. It felt good to let out her pent-up stress, even as a joke. Surprisingly, Allie joined in, howling like a coyote. Liz and Christina joined in, even louder. Kyle howled a fine harmony over Allie's.

"HEY! What the hell is going on in there?" someone yelled from the living room.

"Nothing!" Liz replied innocently, and they all laughed.

Suddenly, the air was split by an off-key Tarzan yell from

the living room.

"Geez, everybody's nuts here," Kyle laughed.

"It's DJ. Jane's out there. It's just something they do."

"*DJ*?"

DJ—a wired, nerdy, twenty-something woman with big glasses—blasted into the kitchen, just in time to hear Kyle mention her name. Immediately likable and slightly awkward—let's say majorly awkward—she sported the latest, not-quite-hip clothing, not quite fitting properly.

"DJ. That's me. Kyle Chandler, I presume." She screeched to a halt and put out her hand quite formally to Kyle. "I've heard nothing about you, but it's all good." Without taking a breath, she switched to a bored Valley Girl accent, "Oh, hi Liz."

"Oh, hi DJ," answered Liz, in the same lame accent.

Both did exaggerated, fake yawns, and then DJ asked, "So, uh. Like, s'up—like?"

"Uh, nothin'. Oh, yeah, like, uh, I'm leaving tomorrow."

"WHAT?" Feigning anguish, DJ stabbed at her heart, fell to her knees, and clung to Liz' leg, babbling unknown words in an unrecognizable accent.

"Later, DJ. C'mon, it's time to eat." Liz grabbed DJ up by the shirt and headed for the dining room. She nodded to Kyle to bring the salad and called everyone to dinner.

Afterward, the women talked over dessert. Clearly, Liz had gathered a group to meet Kyle that regularly partied as comfortable, close friends. Without planning to, they sat around the living room in a rough circle. Allie sat on the couch, with Christina on the floor between Allie's legs. Allie unconsciously stroked her hair. Kyle sat on the floor across from them, saying nothing, watching the women who would become her friends.

Out of the blue, Jane asked, "So Kyle, tell us about yourself. Liz says you're a musician—and you're single?"

Several women winced, including Kyle, who remembered the long ago and far away toasts at the bar.

All Kyle said was, "Uh, yeah."

DJ jumped in. "Everybody got that? Okay. Now, relax Kyle. This won't hurt a bit. We're just going to pick your brain a little. Absolutely routine. I had a lobotomy here last week and didn't even feel it..."

Not to be deflected, Jane continued, "I just wondered if Kyle's gonna join us in the wild world of dating..."

DJ interrupted, "You forgot wezbian."

"Shut up, DJ," said Jane.

Kyle said, "I don't even know what dating means..." and then regretted it. She could have just said, "Yes," and then asked about where to go hiking.

Christina laughed, "Oh, no. Here we go again."

DJ said, "Let's get serious." Everyone looked at her skeptically. "Dating's just a compatibility experiment that ends—or maybe begins—with sex. Dating is also dinners, movies, softball, texting all day, obsessing on your look...

Allie took the bait, "Softball?"

"Yeah! It's a tribal thing, Allie. Everybody loves softball players. Probably what attracts Christina to you...I mean *look* at you."

Everyone laughed as Allie took mock offense. She was a *very* attractive woman.

Liz jumped in, "C'mon, DJ. I hate to bring up the C-word..."

DJ said, "I can't believe that *you*, of all people, are about to say *cunt*."

Liz interrupted the interruption, "No, *commitment*, bonehead. Let's talk commitment."

"Listen, I asked Kyle a simple question about dating," Jane complained.

But Liz was into it. "C'mon, Allie. What do you think? Let Kyle know what she's in for..."

Allie shrugged, but Christina jumped in.

"Okay, here's what I think. Dating is different for every woman. So of course no one agrees. It depends on what each one is looking for. Whatever, it's okay—as long as a woman tells you what she wants."

DJ said, "Like is she trying to get into your pants?"

"They all are. That's not the point," said Christina.

Everyone laughed. Kyle relaxed. She knew she was off Jane's hook.

Christina continued, "So one woman is dating to find sex. Another one wants love. And then there's the big one--the commitment thing like Liz said, partnership, marriage, whatever you call it."

DJ said, "Where were you after they showed *Your Vagina and You* in 5th grade?

Now even Jane was into it. "Keep goin' Chris. What about the woman who just wants sex..."

"Okay. She wants a lover for one night or one year. But she never gives herself."

Judi said, "Whoa, I've met that one!"

Jane laughed, "I probably *am* that one!"

Christina said, "Totally fun if both agree."

"What about love?" Liz asked.

"Okay," Christina went on, "Another woman wants love.

She loves different women over time or..."

Jane laughed, "One at home and one on the side?"

Christina nodded, "Or, she might be open with two lovers or a group—keeping it fresh, spreading the love."

Raz said, "But, is she in love with the women or the drama?"

"Maybe her best friends are down...uh, literally." Liz laughed, "C'mon, no judgment!"

Christina said, "I don't know. I'm not her. I'm the one who wants a mate."

A murmur rippled through the group.

"I did not say husband."

"I found that out," Allie admitted.

Everyone laughed.

Christina continued, smiling at Allie, "I want *this* one, all the time."

Allie said, "I'm her sex toy."

Christina replied, seductively, "Yes, for sex." Then, overdramatizing, she put a hand over her heart, "And for love!"

Liz ventured, "And commitment?"

Allie jumped in, "It gels way before anyone talks about commitment. You know you're one. You can't imagine being apart. *Then* you talk."

Christina continued, "First there's chemistry. Then love."

"And respect," Allie added.

"And trust," Christina continued, "And then, some kind of *alchemy*..."

Allie said, "Yeah, *alchemy*. She pushes all your buttons. You go through heaven and hell, and keep coming back..."

"For the next—what would you call it?—revelation of love," Christina finished.

Suddenly there was silence, and everyone took a breath. *Revelation of love...* Kyle thought. *Where did that come from?*

Allie took Christina's hand. "You see why I love her?"

Mischievously, but with a straight face, Jane turned again to Kyle. "So, Kyle, are you gonna be dating in Tucson?"

This time they all laughed.

Kyle said, "After this, I wouldn't miss it for the world."

- 10 -

The morning Liz left for San Diego, Kyle freaked out. The fact that she was now in Tucson—alone—for ten weeks—hit her like the line drive she missed in fourth grade. Her nose still had a tiny bump where the hard hit ball had broken it. The boys were worried about her, and did not laugh, which was amazing. *She* laughed it off like a good male, and didn't cry a single tear. Despite an advancing headache trying to break through her skull, she finished the game. Unaware of her grossly swollen face, she arrived home for dinner but got an emergency visit to the doctor instead.

Why am I always plagued with memories, even here, in a brand new place? She walked through each room of the unfamiliar but cozy house, seeing way too clearly. Everything was surreal. The empty dining room, overgrown with plants. Two empty coffee cups on the wooden table. A foot-long cactus, thin as a finger, growing in a terra cotta fish planter on the windowsill. *A cactus in a fish...?*

The tiny kitchen. Iron frying pans in different sizes hanging over an old gas stove. Faded linoleum from the seventies curling up at the doorway. A few pellets of cat food near Ratty's dishes, waiting to be stepped on. Kyle opened all the cabinets, painted clean white. Nothing was where she would have put it. She found the silverware drawer, took out a spoon and put it back. *What the hell was she doing here, anyway?*

Breaking her fall into oblivion, Kyle got busy. She took the whole day to unpack, move things around, and make the place her own. Rat came and went through an open window at least a hundred times, apparently doing the same thing. In the afternoon they both took a long nap on Liz' big, comfortable bed that was now theirs.

That night, Kyle stood clean and naked, surveying her clothes. She was going to meet DJ at Tucson's lesbian bar. It was good to have somewhere to go. But what to wear? Not the new boots. Too shiny. Maybe too corny. Better to err on the side of simplicity. She put on a pair of ripped cutoffs, an old white T-shirt, and super cheap flip-flops. Maybe too simple and beachy for Tucson. She had seen better-dressed homeless women in San Diego. She changed back into wrinkled jeans and a semi-wrinkled, worn-in shirt and checked the mirror. *Pretty good. At least it's me.* She looked into her own eyes. A glint of fear reflected back.

Oh, come ON. Don't start that what-am-I-doing shit again. She headed out and locked the door behind her. *Why didn't Nandi come?* She hadn't gone to a bar alone since...since she couldn't remember. Her hands were sweaty. She didn't know anyone. She laughed at herself. Age fifteen revisited.

As she approached the door to Hers, Tucson's women's bar, Kyle adjusted her attitude, adding a veneer of self-confidence over her well-worn, everyday armor. *Get it together, dude. It's just a bar.* She had long ago decided that it was better to appear aloof than reveal the naked terror underneath.

Kyle paused in the entryway as the door closed behind her. Hers was busy but not packed, new but not intimidating, a down home place, mostly wood and leather. A warm, low light illumined the long, mesquite bar. Music blared. Couples glittered in the revolving lights on the dance floor. Kyle relaxed a notch. *Okay, it IS just a bar.*

From the booth above the dance floor, DJ saw Kyle immediately and waved her to come up. Kyle headed up with casual authority, like she'd been there a hundred times before. She avoided all the eyes that turned in her direction.

Oh, NO. As she passed the bar, Kyle recognized Jane, DJ's so-are-you-gonna-be-dating friend, waiting to order drinks. Lighting up, Jane turned to give Kyle a hug. Stiffly, Kyle returned the gesture. She was relieved to actually see someone she knew. But not *that* relieved.

"Kyle! Welcome! Let me buy you a drink."

"No, thanks." Kyle suspected the ice treatment was the only *No* this woman would understand.

"What do you want, a beer? What kind?" Jane persisted. She was standing well within what Kyle considered her personal space.

Heads turned in their direction. Kyle had to get away. "Okay, Corona with lime."

Just then, DJ changed songs and some of the dancers left the floor, opening a straight path to the deejay's booth beyond. Kyle quickly escaped, hoping Jane would forget the beer.

"Great timing on that transition!" she said, taking a chair next to DJ.

DJ beamed, "Be with you in a second."

Looking down, Kyle could see every inch of the bar. Yet, she was inconspicuous, almost invisible, herself. It was every woman's dream. There was an eclectic mix of Anglo, Latina and African-American women, university students, lipstick lesbians, cowgirls, leather girls—all ages, sizes, everything. Two-thirds of a softball team were doing pitchers of beer. If fate ordained it, everyone *could* cross paths in a one bar town like Tucson.

DJ took off her phones and pushed them onto her neck. "You like it so far?"

"Yeah! Cute deejay. Nice lesbiance."

DJ grinned. "I break in fifteen. Watch this. Let's see if they can handle it..."

From rap to disco, DJ now made an amazingly smooth transition into a country two-step. She obviously loved her job. Skilled and intuitive, she was more a mad music scientist than a deejay. Lots of women danced, riding the exciting, unpredictable waves.

Kyle leaned forward to watch the women dancing. With the switch to country, more tight jeans and boots appeared on the dance floor. Kyle enjoyed the view. Hopeful excitement flowed through her body, replacing her initial fear.

At that moment, a Latina couple danced into Kyle's awareness. She was transfixed by the grace and beauty of a woman in the arms of an Amazon. She was smiling, magnetic, and effortlessly seductive. *What if that smile was for me?*

What if she smiled at me, moaned for me, making love? What is it about her? The couple was double-timing and elegantly turning every few steps. Kyle was mesmerized. She didn't know how to two-step. She wanted to be dancing. With that woman.

"Hey, DJ. You know them? See that woman in the white shirt? Long hair..."

DJ was getting the next CD ready.

"DJ!!"

DJ pulled aside one earphone. "Yeah?"

Kyle pointed, "You know them?"

DJ said, "One minute..."

Now, the larger woman was leaning into her partner's space, whispering. Responsive, the beautiful woman listened, apparently enraptured, then threw back her head and laughed unselfconsciously. An electric current ran through Kyle's body. She suddenly filled with joy, with the woman's happiness, and the partner's happiness. She saw herself dancing with this amazing woman, in place of the Amazon, whispering, making her laugh, caressing her face, her neck...

"Kyle, take this!" Jane demanded. She held a coke and two Coronas in a triangle balanced against her body, and shoved the nearest beer toward Kyle.

Kyle took the beer, abruptly thanked her, and turned away to locate the couple dancing.

"DJ!" Jane yelled across Kyle, extending the coke.

But, DJ was still in the midst of a fancy transition. Jane stretched herself across Kyle to put down DJ's coke, obstructing Kyle's view. Kyle went crazy. Having lost sight of the perfect woman, Kyle instinctively stood up, grabbed Jane's back center belt loop and pulled her forcefully out of the way.

Jane laughed, pressing herself against Kyle. Misunderstanding the situation entirely, Jane read Kyle as fabulously flirtatious and funny as opposed to majorly annoyed and preoccupied.

Dammit! Kyle relocated the couple, who were now leaving after the last song. They were at the end of the bar, talking with a woman near the exit. Kyle considered going down there, but what would she say?

Instead, she yelled, "DJ!!!!"

"Okay, where's this couple?"

Kyle pointed. "At the end of the bar, heading for the door. Beautiful woman. White shirt. Amazon with the long braid down her back...."

DJ shook her head. "Don't know them, but I really can't see..."

"Never mind. They're gone." Kyle said, as if she had lost her only chance at happiness.

"Sorry we lost them," said DJ, sincerely. "Next time, rip the phones off my head and throw them into the crowd. Or..."

"Lost who?" Jane interrupted.

"Kyle was checking somebody out."

Jane grabbed Kyle's hand. "C'mon, Kyle. You can check out the local talent while we dance. I won't be possessive."

Kyle shook her head *No*.

Irritated, Jane turned on her heel to leave. "You two are so lame. I'm gonna dance. You're welcome for the coke, DJ. Ditto, Kyle!"

"Thanks," said Kyle, trying not to encourage her.

"Don't mention it!" said DJ.

Jane gave DJ an evil look and headed for the dance floor. DJ laughed and cranked up the music.

"C'mon, Kyle. Everything's on automatic for fifteen," said

DJ, getting up. "Let's go outside. Maybe we can catch your Mystery Woman out there."

Kyle followed DJ out into the cool, clear night air. Expecting nothing, she scanned the empty parking lot for any sign of the lost couple. Of course, they were already gone.

"It was no big thing," said Kyle, already minimizing her experience. "She was with another woman, anyway."

During DJ's next set, Kyle felt much more at home, much more herself. She expertly ditched Jane *again*, had a beer, danced with two cute women, and left in a little over an hour. She had one woman's phone number, which might come in handy some day, and directions to the other's apartment, which she followed immediately.

- 11 -

At the first opportunity, DJ took Kyle for an early morning hike. As they drove north, out of the city into the foothills, rabid workaholics were already speeding by in the opposite direction.

By seven, the two women headed into Sabino Canyon. The main trail led up a gentle hill through an expanse of golden desert dotted with tall cactus and scruffy mesquite trees. Pastel mountains loomed ahead in the distance. To the east, the hour-old sun climbed in a cloudless sky. DJ set a healthy pace and Kyle fell into stride. It was good to be moving, great to be alive.

Halfway up the hill, DJ put out her hand for Kyle to stop. She pointed to a bosque of mesquite trees on their right. Kyle looked for a moment, seeing nothing but trees. Then, the graceful figures of two mule deer emerged from the background. Perfectly camouflaged, they were breakfasting on the long grass beneath the trees. Down wind, DJ and Kyle watched them for a long time.

From then on, Kyle noticed intense movement everywhere-- prairie dogs, jackrabbits, generic big and little lizards, lots of birds. *How do they survive in this harsh place?*

At the top of the hill, the wide desert opened out into a magnificent canyon, with rocky cliffs rising on either side. A small stream meandered through the canyon, a runoff of melted snow from the mountains above. Big, green cottonwoods and willows towered over the water, marking its course. Near the stream, it was shaded, dark, and immensely quiet, except for the faint sound of the stream and the wind rustling through the trees.

"Amazing," said Kyle, reverently.

"Kind of takes you by surprise, doesn't it?"

Kyle followed DJ down an auxiliary trail to walk along the stream. Deep in the canyon, it was still before dawn, and morning mist still hovered over the water. The cool breeze carried pungent smells of ferns and grass, mossy rocks and wet dirt. When they came to a quiet, shaded pool, DJ and Kyle took off their packs, sat on a rock, and opened a thermos of coffee. They settled back to watch everything around them slowly light up and change colors as the sun rose over the canyon wall. Kyle tossed a pebble in the water. Little brown fish scattered and came back, even before the pastel ripples were gone.

"Did you get settled in?" asked DJ.

"Yeah, sort of." Kyle answered. "I might even have a job."

"That was fast."

"I don't know yet. I just talked with the guy at Music City yesterday."

"Awesome! Little Joe, right? Semi-god, works out, alien hand gestures—totally insecure…"

Kyle laughed. "Yeah, that's him."

"By night, he's Miss Tall Tail. Does Beyoncé and Broadway."

"No!"

"Un-huh. That's why he took to you, obviously."

Kyle laughed and shook her head.

"Must take about a size eighty-two pump. But, listen, wait'll you see his basement. I mean literally. Full of unbelievable shit. Guitars, drums. Ten-dollar toy pianos mixed up with vintage Rhodes. What's your job?"

"Part time counter, plus whatever synth lessons I can get. I'll know in a few days."

"Did you play for him?"

"Yeah. The door was open, right? As soon as I started the *Star Wars* theme, two young guys came in off the street and I gave them a free lesson."

"He'll call you."

They headed out again along the creek until DJ took an upward fork. Soon they were back on the main trail, climbing up the canyon into the mountains. Kyle took in the unfamiliar landscape with all her senses. Every so often, DJ would play the tour guide, but mostly they walked easily, without talking. Already comfortable with each other, they were going to be great friends.

Kyle loved the giant saguaros that guarded the cliffs. They were much bigger than they looked in the movies. The old ones with lots of arms each had a distinct personality. Cactus wrens darted in and out of holes in their trunks where their nests were hidden. One wren stood on top of a huge saguaro and sang a long, warbling song. Another bird answered from across the canyon.

DJ stopped at a rocky bend in the trail, and said, "Hey, check this out."

A tiny mesquite tree, maybe a foot tall, was growing directly out of a crack in sheer rock. Both women took a drink of water and marveled at the tenacious tree. *How did it get there? What's keeping it alive?* Kyle carefully poured some water onto its roots.

DJ added some of hers. "I always do it, too."

"Makes you realize how easy your life is," Kyle mused.

"No shit."

In half a mile, they reached a natural lookout, the highest point they would go that day. It was already getting hot. They sat and rested under an eight-foot mesquite that looked out over the canyon and the meandering creek.

DJ said, "Amazing, isn't it?"

Kyle said, "Yeah, it's weird. Harsh and rugged and beautiful all at the same time."

"People either love it or hate it. It sounds like you're gonna love it."

"Well, you've got it all, DJ—hiking by day. Women at night..."

"Yeah, but I need to *meet* some women, Kyle. Nobody notices the adorable yet lonely DJ, high above the crowd. Maybe sometime we could seek out some wine, women, and song together…"

Kyle said, "Of course, we would be irresistible…"

"Your style and my charisma," DJ vogued.

"...But let's not."

"But, Kyle, Liz kind of...suggested...that you, um, find everyone irresistible...and as a musician, you know, you could take advantage of groupies and whatnot."

Kyle just laughed. How did DJ manage to throw *whatnot* into that convoluted sentence, if you could even call it a sentence?

"Oh, sure. I'm star quality, alright. If I'm lucky, my glamorous gig in Tucson will be Music City, selling keyboards."

"Maybe you'll write some new songs this summer and I know some musicians..."

"I haven't written any music in two years..."

"Okay, got it. So forget song. That leaves wine and *my* personal favorite."

"There's no future in women either, DJ. Not for me."

"Jesus, Kyle! Carpe Diem! You could be the biggest thing to hit the desert since rain. You have that wet and wild look about you..."

"Yeah, right. Crazy Jane thinks I'm hot."

"Kyle, this is bigger than your cynical, puny, little conscious mind can grasp. This calls for..." She looked heavenward and fluttered her eyelids rapidly. "Yes. Come in, Madame Lezbee."

Suddenly, DJ pulled her T-shirt back over her head, leaving just her face sticking out. It did look something like a turban. Maybe a cross between a turban and a nun's hat, whatever that's called. She sat cross-legged now, in just her white undershirt stretched tight over bony ribs and small breasts, looking absolutely ridiculous, if not insane. DJ shook her head a few times, flapping the T-shirt behind her, then put out her hands, palms up. Kyle bent over laughing.

In a weird accent, DJ said, "Greetings. Madame Lezbee will now contact her crystal ball and spirit guides." She shaped her hands over an imaginary globe and petted it gently. "Come in, Amazonia, my wise one. Yes, oh, yes! Is Doo-bee also there? Good!"

Kyle laughed. She loved this woman.

DJ leaned back, eyes wide, as if a startling scene had just come into view."Amazonia says she will dispel your stupidity, Kyle, and build up your confidence. Madame Lezbee will show you your past, and then tell your fortune for the summer. Ooohh. Madame Lezbee sees many women. Am I right so far? Uh-huh. Does the name Lydia ring a bell? Lots of tattoos?"

Kyle laughed, "No."

"Honey Lamb Kowalski?"

"Nope."

"Apple-Betty-Caramel-Candy?"

"Not in this lifetime."

"Amazonia, please. Yes, I know she laughed at us. But Kyle's love life is not a joke."

"It is a joke, DJ. She's right about that."

"Wait a minute. Ah-ha. Now Amazonia is coming clear. Madame Lezbee sees a special one with you, Kyle. Very beautiful. Short dark hair. Deep dark eyes...You seem to be having..."

Inexplicably, Kyle leapt to her feet. "Fuck you, DJ! What I told Liz about Jessie was supposed to be private. It's not funny. Go to hell!" Kyle grabbed her pack and took off.

"Kyle, wait!" DJ reeled from the blast.

Kyle stomped down the trail, and then broke into a run.

Running after her, while awkwardly fighting with her t-shirt, DJ yelled, "Kyle! Stop! I was making it up..."

Luckily, Kyle dropped her water bottle out of the half-open pack and had to stop to pick it up. DJ caught up with her.

"I was making it up. Honest," she said, finally getting her t-shirt over her head.

Kyle shot her a fierce look, hurt and angry. But she could see DJ was telling the truth. And she looked so silly and contrite, Kyle tried hard not to laugh and embarrass her even more.

"Dammit!!" DJ self-consciously pulled her T-shirt down over her skinny chest. Unable to stop herself, Kyle burst out laughing.

"Whatever I said, I'm really sorry." DJ didn't want to lose this friendship with one of her stupid moves. "Liz never said anything. Madame Lezbee never heard of…of…what's her name."

Now DJ had to laugh, too, at how stupid that sounded.

"What an idiot," Kyle muttered as they walked back to the point to retrieve DJ's pack.

"I know," said DJ quietly.

"Not you," Kyle reassured DJ.

And then, completely out of character—and out of control—Kyle began to cry. DJ approached and cautiously put her arm around Kyle's shoulder.

"She ditched me two years ago. I guess I'm still a little bent."

"Sorry, Kyle."

"I think about her all the time."

"I'm…sorry. I was just being stupid."

"You were being hysterical. I love Madame Lezbee." Kyle blew her nose in her bandanna and pulled herself together. "You got Jessie right on, though. That was freaky."

"Madame Lezbee has never ever been accurate before," DJ admitted. "I just took a buckshot chance at hitting *something*. There are so many dykes out there with short hair and dark eyes..."

"Let's forget it," said Kyle, with as much "normal" in her voice as possible. She had already composed herself again—into the hurt, angry person she currently recognized as herself. "Aren't you *hungry,* DJ?"

"Famished. C'mon, I know a shortcut back to the car."

Kyle followed DJ down the trail. "Hey, DJ."

"Yeah?"

"Don't mention this, okay?"

"You got it."

"And you know, maybe we should tear up this town together. Why not?"

- 12 -

*D*earest-No News-Not There-Grrlfriend,
   Glad you and Jackie are good. But you are in DEEP SHIT if you send me another goddam generic text! I want all the dish about you. And Kay and Liz and everybody. Write me a decent message! Or pick up the friggin' PHONE!
   I miss you horrenditiously, monstermissingly!
   Liz' friends are cool, but there's nobody like you.
   Tell Liz that DJ and I are already good pals. We went hiking at 6:30 a.m.! I saw deer and movie cactus and NO rattlesnakes. Starting country-dance lessons with Allie. You'd love her. There are some VERY cute women at the bar. (Stop laughing about me doing country dancing, right now!)
   Today, I started work at Music City. Yup, tacky. Actually a

dump. Thurs.-Sat. I do the counter with Little Joe (Big Flaming Queen!) plus keyboard demos, leading to whatever synth lessons I can get. Joe and I are gonna be fabulous together. He's huge, geekily handsome, jeans way too tight, sentimental as hell. Does Beyoncé drag as his main shtick. If she worked out, Adele would be more like it.

First thing on my first day, he puts his arm around me and says, "Kyle, there is just one rule here. An ab-so-lute-ly sacred unbreakable rule." And I start to think Oh, no! Another Nazi boss... And he says, "I wait on all the cute guys. No matter what! No exception. And that's final!" He laughed hysterically and I said, "I get the women." And he said, "That's the deal." It's the classic butch (me) and femme (him) attraction.

The only downside is I've been thinking about Jessie lately—like ALL THE FRIGGIN' TIME! I think about you a lot too. Homesick I guess. Write me SOMETHING, you fickle grrrrl!!! And how about charging your damn cell and using it!!???!!! Hugs to Kay and Liz!
    LOVE!!!!! You better call me.
    K.

- 13 -

It wasn't just because Country Night was a big night for cruising that Kyle found herself in her new black boots at the bar. (She had scuffed them up at home first.) She hadn't told anyone, but she was taking country-dance lessons in case she ever crossed paths with Mystery Woman at the bar. Allie wanted to learn too. So here they were in the back row, behind a dozen women, about to learn the latest line dance. Nandi should see her now!

Any line dance was new to Kyle, but she was determined to try, especially after meeting the cute instructor. Lyndi was the perfect teacher--a gifted dancer, patient mentor, and total flirt. She looked the part in tight jeans, soft western shirt unbuttoned to cleavage, blue boots, and hand-worked silver belt. Kyle imagined her hands all over Lyndi, how beautiful she would be undressed. A natural blond, Lyndi had a shock of long hair in front that she sometimes brushed away from her eyes. On the dance floor, she spoke with undisputed authority.

"Alright, *Ladies*." Lyndi put a twist on *ladies,* so it became an inside joke. "This is just the Slide from last week with a few little changes. Simple. No problem."

Allie turned to Kyle and mouthed the word, "*The Slide*???" Kyle shrugged her shoulders and they laughed like first-graders. It was an ongoing class and they were hitting it cold and ignorant, not to mention awkward and self-conscious.

When Kyle realized she was laughing out loud in a sea of silence, she turned back to Lyndi. Deep in regret, she met the warm brown eyes of her teacher, and was delighted to find them charged with sexiness. There was a hint of a smile on Lyndi's face that seemed to say, *Every class has its bad girls, and I do love bad girls.*

"Watch this, and then we'll break it down," Lyndi continued, directly to Kyle, then finally looking around the class. "Ready?"

She linked her thumbs through her front belt loops, with her fingertips resting on the fly of her 501's. Again, she looked directly at Kyle, as if to keep her attention. By now, Kyle was definitely paying attention. Lyndi nodded to DJ to roll the music. No music. DJ was schmoozing with a cute little wiry dyke in the deejay's booth.

"DJ!" Lyndi yelled. It was amazingly loud in the quiet bar.

DJ leaned out of the booth and whined, "Make her stop it, Kyle!" She was on to the flirtation and was now helping Kyle make the most of it.

"Kyle is *trying* to pay attention," admonished Lyndi, happy to learn Kyle's name.

"Oh, *sorry, Kyle*." said DJ. "Teacher's pet."

"DJ, will you just play the song?" said Lyndi, leaning back on one leg and putting a hand on her hip. To say that Kyle noticed would be a gross understatement. The two were now flirting openly. Lyndi struck the pose purely for Kyle's enjoyment, although everyone in the class was appreciating it, too.

DJ finally rolled the music. Lyndi talked her way through the sequence a few times. Then, without the music, she demonstrated one step at a time and the class followed. Kyle loved watching Lyndi dance. She was so light, so fluid, so absolutely, naturally, openly sexy. Kyle focused intently, trying to copy her moves. Lyndi would be so beautiful naked. Beautiful and good in bed. Kyle would lean down to kiss her from above, brush Lyndi's open mouth, kiss her lightly, kiss her neck, their breasts touching...

Kyle found herself stepping forward as everyone else stepped back. She lurched back as everyone stamped their feet. Her face turned red and hot. She felt a deep, temporary hatred for the four women in the front row. They already knew most of the sequence and only had to learn one new step. She wondered if Lyndi ever slept with anyone who couldn't dance.

"Okay, we've got it. Now, let's put it together with the music."

Nothing.

"DJ!"

Allie and Kyle echoed, "DJ!!"

The familiar song started and the group nervously sprang into action. From tentative to absolutely clueless, the dancers followed Lyndi as best they could. Miraculously, somewhere at the middle of the song, they all began to fall into step, one by one.

When the song ended, Lyndi beamed. "Good job! Now let's do it again. Relax and have fun with it this time."

In the second go-round, everyone actually looked good. Kyle forgave the front row—and Allie—for improvising fancy, unnecessary turns. Kyle did alright, which for her was a win. They switched to learning the simple two-step with a partner. It was the last time Kyle and Allie would ever try to dance together! At exactly nine o'clock, Lyndi wrapped the lesson. DJ played a two-step and the dance floor filled up. Lyndi went to a table with an entourage of women from the class. It was part of the ritual. Allie and Kyle, new to the scene and hot from dancing, went straight to the bar and ordered a beer.

"Lookin' good out there," Allie smiled.

"Yeah, at the end. You catch on a lot quicker than I do," said Kyle.

"Looks like it's working, anyway."

"You mean Lyndi? Yeah, she's pretty cute. You know her?"

"Yeah. But, let's say she knows a lot of women."

"You?"

"Not my type," Allie replied.

"Just wondering. I thought maybe B.C. You know, before Christina."

"Nope. Uh-oh. Brace yourself."

A short, sweet, but slightly odd-looking woman headed toward them grinning widely. Kyle instinctively dodged her. The woman grabbed Allie into a tight bear hug. Kyle watched, amazed that Allie put up with it.

The woman kept the hug going a long time, patting Allie's

back at the end. When she moved toward Kyle, Kyle stuck out her hand in self-defense.

"Trog, this is Kyle. Kyle, Trog."

"*Trog?*"

"She's making that up. No one calls me that. The name is Maryann Teraglia," Trog said, shaking Kyle's hand way too long. "Wanna dance?"

"No, thanks. We're having kind of a personal chat."

"Okay, maybe later."

Allie watched her leave, then said somewhat sheepishly, "B.C."

"No shit!" Kyle laughed, "She'd fit in great with all of mine."

They drank their beers and talked easily about their lives-- the dance lesson, Trog, Christina, Kyle's new job, and the dish on Lyndi and some of the women at the bar.

Finishing her beer, Allie said, "Gotta go. Your homework tonight is at least one dance with Lyndi." Allie got up to leave, then said incredulously, "God, I'm prophetic! Here she comes..."

"Hey, Allie," Lyndi smiled.

"Hey, Lyndi. Thanks for the lesson."

"You did great. See you next week?"

"Yeah, absolutely. Call me, Kyle."

Allie left, but Lyndi didn't take her seat. Instead, she leaned in against Kyle's leg, making room for the line of cruising women to pass by. She said simply, "Would you like to dance?"

Kyle looked into her warm eyes and melted. She wanted to brush that shock of blond hair away from her eyes, lean forward and kiss her passionately. The woman was so seductive. No holding back. No expectations beyond this moment. Just pure chemistry.

Kyle admitted, "I don't really two-step yet, but..."

Lyndi put two fingers up to Kyle's open lips, stopping her in mid-sentence. Kyle suppressed her first reaction, which was to stroke the back of Lyndi's hand and take her fingers into her mouth. She just smiled, not trying to disguise her interest, and returned Lyndi's gaze. There was a good chance that Lyndi was having the other half of her fantasy.

"You're the lucky winner of tonight's private lesson..." Lyndi flashed a dazzling smile. There was an unmistakable spin on the words *private lesson*. Game on. As DJ changed songs, Lyndi took Kyle's hand and led her into the middle of the dance floor. "Just remember, quick-quick-slow-slow."

Kyle looked around nervously. Expert couples were already dancing past them. "We're okay," Lyndi said. "The fast lane is on the outside. They expect us to be slow in here."

She opened her arms and Kyle stepped into them. Almost the same height, they were a perfect fit. Lyndi caught the beat and talked Kyle through the song. She led firmly, but from the following position so Kyle could get the feel of leading.

Lyndi said, "See those two turning? We're gonna do the same thing. I'll tell you when and what to do. Listen to my body—she pressed Kyle's hand while pulling her closer—and yours."

They circled among the other couples, sometimes turning, sometimes dancing without embellishment, just to get the pattern established in Kyle's body. If Kyle didn't respond, Lyndi pulled her ever closer, helping her read her hands' and hips' commands. They danced every two-step, plus the line dance they had practiced. When DJ finally put on a ballad,

Kyle led. It was a huge relief to be back in charge. Lyndi put her arms around Kyle's neck. Kyle pulled her close, then closer. They melted together, barely moving, nipples hard, clothing damp from dancing. Lyndi stroked the back of Kyle's neck. Kyle's hands traveled her back. She rubbed her cheek against Lyndi's, and then lightly kissed her ear, and her neck. She readjusted their hips even closer, and both let out a single sigh of pleasure.

When the song ended, Kyle whispered, "Come home with me."

Lyndi nodded. "My house, okay?"

"Sure. Let's say goodnight to DJ." Kyle took Lyndi's hand and led her up to the deejay's booth. DJ and the cute, wiry dyke had been expecting them.

"You two heading out?" DJ asked.

"Yeah," said Kyle. "You two have a great night."

DJ answered in a motherly tone, "You too. And, Kyle, remember your dental dam, lube, plastic gloves, tarps, raincoat, vitamins, hair net..."

Kyle laughed and pulled Lyndi away. She knew DJ could go on forever.

DJ called after them, "...Goggles, whipped cream, strawberries, and...Have fun, dear! Call us tomorrow!"

-14 -

Kyle followed Lyndi's pickup through town, then past a few manufactured home communities, and finally down a pot-holed dirt road. It was a warm, clear, balmy night. Moonlit mountains framed the horizon in all four directions. House lights were scattered thin. Cactus country. Horse country. Snake country. Not for the faint of heart. Lyndi turned off the road into a long gravel driveway. Seeing their headlights, a horse and several dogs ran across the yard to wait for Lyndi at the fence.

As Kyle cut her engine, Lyndi came up and warned matter-of-factly, "Close your windows tight so the scorpions don't get in."

Kyle closed them tighter than they had ever been! When

Lovers

she got out of the truck, Lyndi took her hand and they looked up for several moments into the clear, starry sky. The Milky Way streamed overhead, behind a half-full moon. Lyndi made it feel sacred to stop and acknowledge where they were, lucky to be alive, in this magnificent desert. Her piece of desert. She smiled at Kyle and kissed her under the stars. The dogs barked impatiently.

When Lyndi opened the gate, she and Kyle slipped through and were instantly besieged with happy animals. "Hi, guys. Okay. Good girls!" Lyndi said, petting the dogs that wriggled around her. She kind of exchanged breaths with her horse, then rubbed his head. "Beautiful, Jake. My beautiful Jake."

"Okay. Okay. Down. Down!" Kyle waited with the dogs as Lyndi fed Jake. They did settle down, and she petted them absent-mindedly while watching Lyndi. The woman was so wonderful with these animals, so beautifully natural and caring, unafraid of dirt and drool. In total contrast, Kyle couldn't wait to wash her hands. *I'm so lucky to have my own little Rat! Cats are so clean and adorable and unclingy.*

Kyle followed Lyndi into the house, a modified mobile home, along with the dogs. The living room was more than a mess, more than lived in. It was more like a cozy animal shelter. Several dogs and cats jumped off the old furniture to greet Lyndi and Kyle as they entered.

"Hi, sweethearts! I'm home. Who's my baby?"

The biggest dog jumped up onto Kyle's chest, then waggled around her, intent on licking both of her hands. Kyle was not in the mood. "Yes. Okay. Down. DOWN!"

"Abby!" said Lyndi firmly, and the dog immediately chilled. Kyle seriously began to contemplate an escape.

"It's wild, isn't it? I see you're not an animal person."

"I have a cat."

"I have every stray dog and cat in the neighborhood." Lyndi laughed. She took Kyle's hand, and switched to a low, inviting voice, "C'mon, you need to be in the bedroom..."

Kyle followed Lyndi to a door at the end of the hall, wondering what lurked inside. Lizards, snakes, guinea pigs, parakeets? Preparing to bolt, she thought about how to say she wasn't feeling well...But, Lyndi opened the door into a totally different world—admirably clean and quiet, and not an animal or animal hair or dog toy in sight. A very inviting queen bed with a country coverlet. A beautiful, southwestern rug on a dark hardwood floor. A big, overstuffed leather chair and a solid oak bookshelf and desk. All in perfect order, ready for a feature in Architectural Digest. Kyle couldn't hide her amazement.

"Even I have my limit for chaos," Lyndi laughed. "Listen, I've gotta give these guys their dinner. Give me 5 minutes. I'll bring you what? Beer? Wine? Coffee or tea? What?

"A Coke and some water would be great."

Lyndi closed the door behind her and Kyle studied the photos on her desk. One with her dad—a handsome, square jawed Clint Eastwood type, complete with big-buckled rodeo belt, cowboy hat, and boots. One with her mom, a pretty, generic blond with big hair, big boobs and a frilly western blouse--definitely an older and less sophisticated version of Lyndi. One with Lyndi astride the horse outside and a handsome butch woman on a big gray.

Kyle looked at the inviting bed, and then remembered the dog slime on her hands and face. She washed at the bathroom sink, then checked the mirror in front of her. Lyndi stood behind her, smiling back. Kyle laughed, surprised. She hadn't heard her come in.

From behind, Lyndi put her arms around Kyle's waist, pressing her ample breasts into Kyle's back. Then, she stuck out her hands over the sink. "Do mine, too!"

Kyle guided Lyndi's hands under the faucet and somehow got them washed and dried. It was fun and looked funny in the mirror, like a strange Hindu goddess trying to manage her four arms. Reaching from behind, Lyndi's hands found Kyle's belt and loosened it. She lifted Kyle's shirt out of her jeans with one motion. Kyle held her breath, wanting Lyndi to slip her hand into her jeans. She was already wet, anticipating her.

Instead, from behind, Lyndi's hands moved under the open shirt to caress Kyle's stomach. She moved across Kyle's ribs, and the bottom of Kyle's breasts. She cupped a breast in each hand and massaged them while watching Kyle's rising desire in the mirror. She drove Kyle crazy tracing circles around her nipples.

"Ohhh," Kyle sighed, wanting so much more.

They watched themselves in the mirror, Lyndi still leading and Kyle responding, both very hot now, both wanting more. Kyle desperately wanted to free herself to turn and kiss Lyndi. But she allowed herself to be held firmly in place by Lyndi's body, still leaning full length against her, pressing Kyle's thighs against the sink.

"Lyndi," whispered Kyle, leaning back.

Lyndi pulled slightly on the hard tips of both nipples. A thrill of electricity went directly to Kyle's clit. She sighed again, deeply, moving her body against Lyndi's weight, but going nowhere, surrendering. Lyndi took her hands from Kyle's breasts and unhurriedly unbuttoned her shirt, nuzzling behind Kyle's ear as she worked. When Lyndi undid the last button, she held Kyle's shirt open, exposing her to the mirror. She admired Kyle's body, and then looked into her eyes. Longing and desire flowed between them.

Lyndi released her pressure on Kyle's back and legs. She was as needy as Kyle for more intensity. Finally free, Kyle turned immediately and kissed Lyndi hard, Lyndi's mouth open for Kyle's tongue. Kyle's very sensitive breasts pressed against the cold metal snaps on Lyndi's western shirt. She ran her hands through Lyndi's hair, over her cheeks, her neck, and down the front of her shirt as she kissed her. Then in one swift motion, she yanked Lyndi's shirt with both hands and all the snaps ripped open. Kyle kissed Lyndi's neck and breasts as she removed her bra and threw it aside. She pressed herself against Lyndi, skin to skin, breast to breast. They kissed deeply, passionately, leaning into each other, seeking a closer fit.

"Jesus!" Lyndi gasped, finally pulling away from the kiss. Heading for the bed, she beckoned, "Let's get those kick-ass boots off."

Kyle sat down on the bed, leaned back, and stuck out a foot. Lyndi pulled off one boot, and held out her hands for the next. Kyle flashed back to her last night in San Diego at the bar, when she held up the shiny black boots for everyone to see. If those women could see those boots now! She held up her second boot and Lyndi yanked it off. Switching places, Kyle covered Lyndi's breasts with ample kisses, then stood over her and pulled off the dark blue boots. Lyndi opened her 501's and Kyle took them off, revealing black silk boxers underneath.

"I don't believe it!" Kyle laughed, leaving them on.

"Come to bed," Lyndi laughed.

Kyle threw off her jeans and underwear in one motion and came to her waiting lover. She leaned over Lyndi and slowly

Lovers

ran a hand up her inner thigh into the leg of her boxers. Lyndi smiled and lay back, closing her eyes and opening her legs. Kyle's light touch opened Lyndi's inner lips and rubbed the slick wetness over her. Lyndi looked up into Kyle's eyes with keen desire.

Kyle leaned down and kissed her passionately. Her tongue moved around Lyndi's mouth, echoing the movement of her fingers around her clit, teasing the lips of her vagina, and back again. She kissed Lyndi's neck and throat as her fingers drew rhythmic circles, exerting a little more pressure. Moving to Lyndi's breasts, she took the hard nipples in her teeth and pulled, one by one, as she concentrated her pressure exclusively on Lyndi's clit.

Lyndi moaned, "inside. Please. Make me come."

Kyle's fingers entered Lyndi, first slightly, then more forcefully, until she was thrusting deeply and rhythmically. Lyndi suddenly shifted position to put her hand into her boxers. Kyle moved her hand to make room for Lyndi's, still penetrating Lyndi in an unbroken rhythm. Lyndi rubbed her clit and kissed Kyle deeply with total abandon. She came quickly, pulling away from the kiss with a long, happy groan of release. Kyle felt Lyndi's last contractions ripple over her fingers. Once or twice, Lyndi moved against her hand slightly, triggering the last sensations of orgasm. Kyle kissed her face and lips lightly while the sensations subsided. Lyndi sighed deeply, then sat up.

"I guess I couldn't wait," she laughed. "God, I'm thirsty."

She reached up and grabbed the Cokes they had both forgotten, handing one to Kyle. The shift was so abrupt, Kyle wondered if this was the end of lovemaking. She immediately found out.

"I love these old fashioned bottles, don't you?" Lyndi asked, taking a long drink. "Don't they remind you of when you were a kid?"

Kyle was starting to answer when Lyndi rubbed her cold bottle across Kyle's skin, from neck to pubic hair. Kyle involuntarily took a deep breath and stopped whatever she was saying in mid-sentence. A warm, desert breeze from the open window excited Kyle's wet skin and dried it quickly. Lyndi gently cupped one of Kyle's breasts in her hand, and carefully touched the cold bottle to the nipple, which immediately contracted and went hard. Kyle drew in a shocked breath. Lyndi delighted at the effect, and tried it again on the other nipple. Then, she leaned in to retrace the line from her neck to her clit with her tongue. She took a long drink and offered the Coke to Kyle. Kyle was about to speak when Lyndi cut her short with a long, slow, intimate kiss. It made the line of wet skin down Kyle's torso feel like a big neon arrow pointing to her clit, flashing red, then blue, then red.

Lyndi must have read Kyle's mind—or body—because she rubbed the cold bottle up against Kyle's clit a few times, then left it standing between her thighs. Kyle playfully thrust her hips, holding the bottle with her thighs so it behaved like a strap-on. The bottle jiggled and they laughed and got silly. Kyle invited Lyndi to sit on it, but she had a better idea. She took the bottle and downed the last of the Coke. With the last drops still in her mouth, Lyndi stationed herself between Kyle's legs and put her mouth over Kyle's clit. She let the cold liquid roll out, then moved it around with her tongue.

"Ohh," Kyle sighed.

Lyndi sucked in the cool Coke and let it back out over Kyle's clit, just playing. Then, expertly, she licked Kyle for ten minutes of agony and ecstasy, keeping her on the edge of orgasm, until she finally came with a vengeance, moaning and arching her back.

Literally moments later, Lyndi jumped up to get more drinks and some fresh strawberries. *DJ must have known something about the strawberries…*

Kyle lay back, opened her legs to the air, and alternately tightened and let go her pelvic muscles, enjoying the lingering ripples of orgasm and following them like the ring of a bell into infinity. Lyndi was not, apparently, the type to cuddle her lovers through this wondrous experience. Instead, she returned with a huge serving tray and laid out a feast of strawberries, whipped cream, roasted almonds, water, sodas, and brandy. She also opened the cabinet in the headboard above her bed to reveal a museum-worthy collection of sex toys and lube already laid out.

Unbelievable!

Coyotes howled somewhere in the distance. It was a long, wild night.

- 15 -

A fern-draped fountain greeted Kyle at the entrance to the Midtown Greenery, a wonderful meld of coffee house and plant nursery. She followed a winding flagstone walkway, trying not to step on the tiny green plants growing in the cracks between stones. Looking for her friends, Kyle passed quiet couples at tables for two, plus animated parties of ten or twelve, apparently in meetings. Nestled among clustered pots of seedling trees and exotic plants for sale, the whole scene was illuminated by strings of white lights in the mature trees planted through the grounds.

Kyle spotted her group at a big table in back, mostly women from Liz's going-away party. She hadn't seen them together since her first night in Tucson, two weeks—or was it forever?—ago. There was one empty chair waiting for her, between Allie and DJ. Allie had called the pals together to plan their annual, Fourth of July weekend at the beach in Puerto Penasco, Rocky Point. Every year, a different combination of the group went, depending on their current schedules, lovers, and disposable income. Over coffee, the women checked in, then got down to business, figuring out who would be going. Allie and Christina went every year. This year, it looked like Raz and Judi—two singles—were going, along with two other friends. Kyle hesitated. She really wanted to go but had no one to room with. Expense was an issue, and she wondered if a lone wolf would be awkward for everyone. DJ couldn't go, having to work the holiday weekend every year. She didn't want to ask Lyndi. They would be too loud and obnoxious at night, and too sleep deprived during the day...

Before Kyle could decline, Allie said, "So we'll book four rooms. Kyle, if it's okay with you, we'll pencil you in. Somebody always shows up at the last minute. But, if nobody does, we always split the cost of all the rooms anyway, so it'll be no big deal. Probably about eighty bucks for the weekend."

How could Kyle say No? "Wow, that's great. Thanks, everybody!"

She was grateful that the group had embraced her so soon and so completely. She beamed them all a love-filled smile in return.

The holiday weekend shored up, DJ announced that Billie Knight, an icon of women's music, was coming to Tucson on June 25th. DJ offered to get tickets, and Kyle signed on immediately. The date didn't work for anyone else, and Kyle was secretly pleased. It would be phenomenal to go with DJ, a walking encyclopedia of music, who apparently loved Billie as much as she did.

Later, DJ turned to Kyle and said quietly, "You know about Billie's Tucson connection?"

"Connection?"

"Yeah, here's the dish. That woman at the far table over there—talking with the blue-hair couple—owns the Greenery. Grapevine has it that she was once Billie's lover—or may still be, when Billie comes through town. Guess what else? Billie *plays* here on occasion. Just shows up. Free. Yeah, no shit! I caught her once—phenomenal!"

"Wow," mused Kyle. "Without the band?"

"Yup, Billie unplugged…"

"But, this place is like a jungle. How…"

"She plugged in at the greenhouse and sat up there. They open everything up—push back all the pots to set up chairs. And, see? There's already speakers in some of the trees."

"Amazing…"

"Keep your ears open. And, perhaps, when her concert date is closer, we'll consult Madame Lesbee…"

- 16 -

There was nothing but mindless shit on TV. Remote in hand, Nandi was watching all of it five seconds at a time when her cell rang. She clicked off the TV and answered the phone, hoping it was Jackie.

"Nandi! Kyle. I was afraid you'd be out."

"Nope, I'm home tonight, the happy housefrau."

"That sounds nasty."

"Yeah, Jackie's working late again. I ate my homemade lasagna and Caesar salad by candlelight about an hour ago."

"That sounds nasty, too."

"It was. So how's my cowgirl friend? S'up?"

"Nuthin'. I just had to cry on your shoulder. Remember that hot dance teacher I told you about? Lyndi?"

"Yeah, what'd she do now?"

"I went to her place two weeks in a row after class, right? So last night I thought maybe she'd come home with me. I've been having fantasy sex with her all over the house."

"Uh-huh."

"Well, Allie and I peed our pants when she brought this older woman to class—maybe forty, forty-five, totally butch and handsome. Her boots probably cost more than my truck."

"And you have on ripped jeans and a T-shirt with spaghetti sauce on the front."

"Yeah. How'd you know? Anyway, Lyndi introduces her as a master dance teacher from LA and we're so lucky 'cuz she's here and tonight we're going to finesse our two-step."

"Yeah, right."

"The ten takes over the class. She makes a big joke about how many women try to lead while they're pretending to be following."

"How many?"

"All of them. Anyway, I'm thinking, *She's all talk--a ten trying to psych us out.*"

"And?"

"She was phenomenal."

"Oh, no."

"Oh, yes. After the pep talk, DJ played a fast two-step. She led Lyndi through this dazzling routine and everyone could see they must be sleeping together. I mean it was so *beautiful*, so smooth, and Lyndi's almost part of her body. And they're smiling at each other. With all that ten and two chemistry. Broke my heart. After class, Lyndi came over and sweetly said she can't be with me tonight. See you next week. So that's it. My sob story."

"God, what a hopeless, depressing, irretrievable disgusting mess," Nandi joked.

"C'mon Nan, give me some sympathy!"

"Well, how much can you mourn lost lust?"

"A lot."

"Bet you're back in the saddle next week."

"Maybe. Hey, the good news is I'm going to a Billie Knight concert with DJ the week after next."

"Billie Knight? You lucky dog!" Nandi heard Jackie's key in the door. "Hey, here's my woman now. I'll call you tomorrow."

As Nandi hung up the phone, Jackie blew into the apartment, reeking of alcohol. She tossed her briefcase, jacket, and keys on the nearest chair and gave Nandi an obligatory kiss, then stretched out next to her on the couch. Nandi shot her an angry look.

"Oh, geez, Nan. Didn't I tell you I had a business dinner?"

Nandi didn't bother to reply.

Jackie grabbed the remote and turned on the TV.

- 17 -

Kyle and Joe were dusting the instruments at Music City and shining the place up. It was Friday, so every music geek with a paycheck would come by within a few hours. While they worked, Joe told Kyle another convoluted story about his love life. His latest boyfriend had just ended their two-week affair. Surprisingly delicate for a big, burly guy, Joe could have almost any of the tops in town, and that was the problem—he was rapidly going through the list. Again today, he was heartbroken, and Kyle's own broken heart went out to him.

"He was a jerk anyway," said Kyle.

"I know," admitted Joe. "But why do I always fall for them? Oh, never mind. What did you do last night, Ms.

Cool?"

"Nothing."

"Hmm. We're secretive. Must be juicy."

"Okay. I lay on the couch, listened to Emmy Lou Harris, ate junk food, and felt sorry for myself."

"Why are we brooding?"

"Musician thing, Joe. Being sensitive and miserable takes commitment and practice."

"I love you when you're maudlin. Play me a sicko ballad, would you? It'll be good for both of us."

Kyle turned on one of the synths on display and sat down, "Okay, what?"

"You know any Barry Manilow?"

"Oh, gag," Kyle put a finger to her mouth.

"Okay, what about Karen Carpenter? Judy Garland?"

"Okay, I know just the thing..." Kyle said. Selecting a voice called *Blues Piano*, she played a beautiful, heartthrobbing ballad.

Joe held his hand to his heart, "Oh, that's it."

Kyle didn't notice the little bell that rang when the door opened. Joe did. He could hear it over the roar of an airplane engine if necessary.

Joe came over and whispered, "Wrap it up, Kyle. There's a customer. *Definitely* for you."

Joe's reliable gaydar never failed. But he had no idea that the dyke entering his store was a tribal icon. Kyle resolved the song with a melancholy jazz chord and turned around. Billie Knight!!! She leaned on the counter, looking directly at Kyle.

"Really nice," she said, smiling.

"Billie!" she blurted, rushing behind the counter. "You were listening? Amazing. I mean sorry to keep you waiting. What do you need?"

"Two sets of strings. Those, please." Billie pointed.

Kyle put the strings on the counter. "I love your music. I'm coming to the concert..." She looked up and stopped abruptly. Billie was looking right past her.

Billie had noticed the sign posted behind Kyle and read it aloud, "*Keyboard lessons. Performing and composition. See Kyle.* Is that you?"

"Yeah, that's me."

"Was that one of yours, when I came in?"

"Yeah, old tune."

"It's great. Really good. What kind of stuff are you writing now?"

"Now? Uh, nothing really. Used to write, uh, actually a little of everything, and play in a band."

"And now?"

"I don't know. I'm just here for the summer. Band's in San Diego. It's a long story..."

"It's gotta be a woman."

"Yeah."

"Can't cry, can't write?"

"Right. I uh...it just…I've never talked about this before. I just stopped writing. I think it's gone. I hate it."

"I've been there, too. Pure hell. Drank too much for a while. Then learned to stay blank without it."

Kyle couldn't believe Billie—Billie Knight!—knew the same emptiness she felt every day. "Did you...get over it?"

"I fell apart."

Kyle laughed. Billie didn't.

"No, seriously. One day, it all caught up with me. You know what triggered it? *Casablanca.* Figure that out. I started crying at the end, when Elsa gets on the plane, like I always do…But, man, I *cried*. For *hours*. Then off and on for *days*. All my shit surfaced. I cancelled two months of gigs before I pulled myself together. I faced the pain of living outside of love…"

Suddenly, Kyle felt the deep heaviness inside her own heart, pressing against her, crushing her...

"…It's like now you know there's another dimension, a beautiful world, but you're outside. The door's been slammed in your face and locked from inside. And if you don't die from it—or, actually, it's more like if you don't stay dead—the music comes back."

"Wow..."

"It was a long time ago. I've done four albums since then! Hey, I'd better pay for those, okay?"

Kyle was transfixed. She had totally forgotten about Billie's guitar strings. She laughed self-consciously and put Billie's strings in a small bag. "These are on me, Billie. Enjoy!"

Billie accepted with a smile, "Thanks, Kyle. See you tonight."

"Yeah, see you tonight!"

As Billie opened the door and the little bell sounded, Kyle's heart was in her throat with both joy and rekindled pain. "Thanks!" she called after Billie, and then softening, "Thanks for everything."

But, by then, Billie was gone. Kyle kicked herself all day and for many afterward for *not* asking, "*Did love come back, too?*"

- 18 -

Just before seven, Kyle joined DJ in line at the Rialto behind twenty other Billie Knight fanatics. Kyle wanted to tell DJ about meeting Billie, but DJ could create a major scene about it. So, Kyle decided to fill her in later. DJ was full of news anyway, and they easily fell into conversation with some other women in line. When the hall opened, they got great seats in the center-balcony with the best acoustics and an awesome view for people-watching. Soon, the intimate house filled up and buzzed with excitement. Kyle looked for the Mystery Woman from her first night at the bar, and for Lyndi. She didn't see either one, but there were definitely some interesting women out there...

When Billie took the stage, the crowd leapt to its feet,

cheering. Smiling and waving in acknowledgement, Billie picked up her guitar and immediately began the intro to one of her classics. The crowd cheered again. Kyle knew the tune by heart. But, this time it was Billie's essence that she felt and heard. Playful. Vulnerable. Deep. Ecstatic. Kyle noted every wave of emotion that crossed Billie's expressive face. In live performance, she gave every word and every chord progression a new meaning and new life. Even with just guitar and voice, Billie's music was real and raw, huge actually, filling the space even without her band behind her. Kyle flashed back to the mellow, open-hearted Billie she had met at the store. It was amazing to see her now, radiant, emanating her full power, animated by spirit.

Two and a half hours later, it was over, after a phenomenal single set with two encores. Finally, someone turned up the house lights and the last standing ovation died out. Stuck deep in the disbursing crowd, it took Kyle and DJ forever to descend the stairs and reach the lobby where Billie would be signing autographs.

"Geez!" said Kyle and DJ simultaneously as they followed Billie's line past a hundred and fifty women to get to the end.

DJ grumbled, "Is every dyke in the world in line? Are they bussing them in..."

DJ continued talking but Kyle heard nothing. As she turned the corner, Kyle plummeted off her own internal cliff. Her stomach clutched. Red heat flamed into her cheeks. She felt exposed, self-conscious, weak. Directly ahead, Mystery Woman and her dance partner leaned against the wall, talking with a little group of women in line. Kyle had to walk by— somehow. Miraculously, her weak legs did not fail her. She got a closer look as she passed Mystery Woman in slow motion. She took Kyle's breath away. Kyle's heart pounded. She must have been smiling because, from another dimension, the woman noticed her and smiled back with a *Do I know you?* look.

When they reached the end of the line, Kyle excitedly whispered to DJ, "She's here, DJ! Mystery Woman is here! How did I miss her before?"

DJ looked blank.

"Remember? My first night at the bar? I saw her dancing and you called her *Mystery Woman*."

Still blank, DJ replied, "Where is she? Maybe I know her."

"Right near the corner. Long hair. Striped blue shirt. Leather vest. With her Amazon girlfriend. A couple other women…"

Unintentionally looking in the wrong direction, DJ said, "Hmm...”

Kyle grabbed DJ's shoulders and pointed her at the woman. "Behind the redhead."

DJ said, "Oh, *her*. Mmm, no wonder..."

At that moment, the woman turned around and caught them both staring at her. She smiled, amused.

Kyle looked away, horrified. She stepped back against the wall, her face turning a deeper, magnificent red. "God, this is worse than high school!"

"Uh-oh. Now her girlfriend is looking at us," DJ grimaced. "You know, she could kill us both with a single wad of old bubble gum…”

"I'm gonna die. Are they around the corner yet?"

DJ pulled Kyle forward. "They're gone now. It's okay."

Kyle said, "Well, do you know her?"

"Not really. She comes to the bar sometimes. Maybe Allie

Lovers

and Christina know her..."

"No big thing. I just wondered," said Kyle, still embarrassed.

"No big thing, huh? Why are you such a mess?"

By the time they reached the main lobby, Mystery Woman had already left. Simultaneously relieved and disappointed, Kyle turned her attention to Billie. She was graciously treating every woman in line like a good friend. DJ bought her newest CD for Billie to sign, but Kyle already had them all.

Billie was talking with the woman ahead of them when she noticed Kyle. She grinned broadly, still high as a kite from performing, "Hey, Kyle! How's it goin'?"

DJ blurted out, "She *knows* you?"

Moving up in line, Kyle said, "Great! Awesome concert, Billie. This is DJ..."

Tongue-tied, DJ handed her the CD. "I haven't unwrapped it yet."

"That's okay."

"Wait a minute," DJ blurted out, fumbling in her pants pocket. "Got it..." She struggled to open her Swiss Army knife.

Meanwhile, for the sake of the women still in line, Billie went ahead and split the shrink-wrap with a quick move of her pen. She had been through this a thousand times, but not with anyone remotely like DJ.

"Great, you got it," said DJ awkwardly, putting the knife away. "Knife opens hard sometimes, but it's got a great coffeemaker. Chain saw is awesome..."

Billie laughed and signed the CD. "What's DJ stand for anyway?"

"Dumb jock. Family name."

Billie handed it back to DJ. "Great to meet you. Thanks for coming tonight."

DJ beamed and just stood there.

"You were brilliant, fantastic, mind-blowing!" Kyle moved up to shake Billie's hand. Instead, Billie leaned over the table for a hug. "Take care, Kyle. And write!"

DJ couldn't believe it. Before they even got to the door, she grabbed Kyle's arm and exploded, "Jesus, Kyle! Why didn't you *tell* me? You *write* to her?"

Kyle pushed her out the door.

- 19 -

Blinding light. An open field, surrounded by pine forest. Sun shimmering on tall grass, gold then green, then gold. White and gold wildflowers moving almost imperceptibly in a light, gentle breeze. Sweet dance of palpable joy.

Kyle emerged out of the forest, coming to meet her lover in this magical place. But, Jessie was nowhere in sight. She called her name expectantly, then frantically, "Jessie! Jessie!"

Like the answer to a prayer, Jessie walked out of the forest toward Kyle. Smiling. Eyes full of love. Brushing the tall grass with one hand as she passed. Shirt casually slung over her shoulder. Loose shorts around her hips. Long, long legs. The flowers were dancing! The field was dancing!

Kyle ran to meet her, feeling strong, light, invincible, almost flying.

"Jessie!"

In Jessie's arms again. Kissing Jessie again. Love flowing through her body again. She lay down with Jessie on a blanket in the grass. They undressed each other slowly, kissing newly exposed breasts and thighs as if for the first time. The sun warmed their skin and the breeze cooled it. A liquid light flowed through Kyle's body to Jessie and back, circling through endless kisses, their hands and hearts deep inside each other, until the unbearable explosion into pure joy. Bodies still trembling, satisfied, they lay in each other's arms and fell asleep.

Kyle suddenly woke up, her skin very cold. Jessie was gone. Kyle looked for her across the field, but it had now faded into an impenetrable fog. She could barely see to pull on her clothes.

She panicked, calling "Jessie! Jessie!"

No answer.

Running blindly into the dark forest, feeling her way forward from tree to tree, Kyle stopped herself at the edge of a cliff, her eyes tearing at the cold wind blowing relentlessly into her face. In the distance, the fog thinned in several places, revealing a beach far below. There, Jessie walked along the shore alone, away from Kyle. Kyle called Jessie's name into the wind, but her voice made no sound. Below, the beach—and Jessie—disappeared into the fog.

Kyle made her way down a steep path toward the beach, cutting her hands and legs on the rocks, not noticing, not feeling anything except fear. At the bottom, the beach was empty in all directions, appearing and disappearing in the moving fog. Kyle ran along the shore where Jessie had last disappeared, and the wind pushed back against her.

"Jessie!" The roar of the wind and breaking surf swallowed her name.

Kyle stopped to breathe, her chest heaving for air. There was no more beach, just black rocks and ocean now. Angry waves splashed against her legs. She set her feet in the sand against a powerful undertow. There was nothing but the rising black ocean, the dark, jagged cliffs appearing and disappearing in the fog, and the relentless wind. The wind howled, whipping her wet clothes and hair. Kyle lifted her head to the sky and screamed. She heard nothing, yet screamed again and again.

Kyle woke up screaming, "Jessie!" at the top of her lungs. She sat up abruptly and Rat flew off the end of the bed.

Terrified and covered with sweat, Kyle turned on the light. Variations of this dream had plagued her before, but never as real as this, never waking her up with her own anguish. She began to cry, desperately, uncontrollably. It was more than grieving or heartache or loneliness. Beyond emotions, her body sobbed with its own sorrow that had to be thrown off and cleansed with tears. She cried long after her eyes hurt and her head ached and she couldn't breathe. The crying had a life of its own. She had always been afraid of her pain for this reason, afraid it was endless, afraid it would take over her life forever.

She couldn't fight it any more.

Hours later, when the tears finally subsided as naturally as they had come, Kyle was amazed. Like the last black cloud of a violent storm passing over, the storm had finished its life cycle. She felt exhausted and clean. She had forgotten that it used to work this way as a child.

At some point, Rat had returned to be with Kyle. He was

now playing cat hockey with one of Kyle's used Kleenex on the floor. Kyle picked it up, along with the million used Kleenex strewn everywhere, and threw the whole mess out. She went to the bathroom to splash gallons of cold water on her face. She looked into her red, puffy eyes in the mirror. God, she looked horrible!

Four a.m. Too messed up to go to sleep, Kyle put some water on to boil for a cup of chai. Rat rubbed against her legs. Kyle rolled a couple cat treats across the floor and Rat was off. Waiting for the water, Kyle noticed a haunting melody running through her mind. A real torcher. Some old classic. What was it? She scanned her memory, suddenly realizing it was new. Hers!

She took her tea to the synthesizer and began to pick out the melody. She tentatively sang whatever words came as she worked. When she had the basic arrangement on the synth, she took a pad to the table and wrote the lyrics. By the time the windows turned a pastel blue, she was finished. She wrote *World of Dreams* across the top of the page and read through it one last time.

World of Dreams

When the wild wind calls your name
And nothing in the world is what it seems
Then I long to run and catch you, hold you
Beyond the world of dreams

When the wild wind calls my name
In the mirror, I see you in my eyes
Then I long to run and catch you, hold you
Before the vision dies

Thank you for opening my mind, love
But now there's nothin' left to believe
Thank you for opening my heart, love
But you're takin' it all when you leave

When a woman calls my name
And I touch her, I see you in her eyes
Then I long for you to touch me, hold me
Before the vision dies
Before the last good-bye.

Much earlier, Rat had tired of playing with the crumpled pages on the floor and was fast asleep. One or two birds sang in the pre-dawn stillness. Kyle was spent. She fell into bed and into a deep sleep that lasted 'til noon.

- 20 -

Still running, Nandi opened the garage door to Jackie's condo from a distance, revealing Jackie's BMW on one side and Michelle's new doghouse, dishes, and toys on the other. She took Michelle off her leash as the door buzzed down behind them. Miraculously calm after the run, Michelle ran to her water bowl and drank like a champion. Nandi bounded into the condo, eager to see her lover.

Jackie yelled, "Hey," but didn't look up from her mail.

"Hey," Nandi replied seductively, as she sat playfully on Jackie's lap.

"Nandi, we need to talk," Jackie said overly-seriously, ignoring the gesture, and throwing her mail on the table.

Nandi moved onto the couch close to Jackie. She

maintained her own carefree mood, with or without Jackie's participation. She had developed this important survival mechanism after moving in. Earlier in their relationship, she would have been devastated by Jackie's indifference.

"Listen, I just got a call from my friend, Barbara Davis..."

Nandi stiffened and pulled away. "The LA bitch. Spare me the details."

"I can't. She was at the airport. She's coming here."

"What? Are you out of your *mind*?"

"She's here on business."

"Not *my* business. You can fuck around in LA if you want, but..."

Jackie interrupted. "She's gonna be staying here."

"No way!!" exclaimed Nandi, totally off-center.

"This *is* my house." Jackie was acting like this was no big deal, like it wasn't asking Nandi for the impossible. This was not going to be a threesome, even if Nandi were interested.

Nandi just looked at her, totally in shock.

"She's already on her way. She's covering a client for another partner who's sick..."

"Jackie, if she's not important to you..."

"I didn't say she wasn't important. I said it doesn't matter."

"You're so twisted. You're *sleeping* with her."

"Well, where's she gonna stay? You know I stay with her in LA. She's gotta stay here. You...can have the guest room." Jackie's sick genius almost made it sound logical. "It's no big deal. She'll be gone in two days."

"*Two days!*" Nandi blurted out. Tears rushed into her eyes and she bolted for the bedroom. She wiped her tears on her running shirt and hurriedly stuffed some clothes into her duffel bag. No time to change—she needed to be gone before the bitch arrived. She didn't want to see her or know anything about her. That was more than she could bear.

Nandi's phone rang and clicked into message mode. It was Kyle.

"Girlfriend! Call me. Billie Knight was awesome. Hey, I actually wrote a song last night! Call and I'll play it for you. Loved your email. Glad things are good with you and Jackie. Bye."

- 21 -

The minute Kyle dismantled Music City's old window display, she started getting personal phone calls. It was the worst possible timing. Joe hated it when chaos took over the front window, however briefly. Even worse, it all started with a call for her on the business line. Joe *thought* he was keeping the business line clear in case his latest trick forgot his cell number.

When the phone rang, he jumped to grab it, cooed a theatrical, "Music City," then gushed with a dazzling, evil smile, "Phone for you, *Princess*."

Joe punctuated his displeasure by waving the phone dramatically in several directions like a drag queen perched in a Pride Parade convertible. A pink or robin's egg blue convertible. With a young, shirtless, muscle-bound sex object in sunglasses driving.

"Music City. This is Kyle."

"*Princess?* This is DJ, your royal..."

Kyle laughed, "Oh, no. No way. Don't you *dare* start calling me Princess! And why are you calling on the business phone? Be fast. Joe's gonna freak."

DJ ordered a mic cable for the bar so it was legitimate. But, she was really just checking in with her romance guru. She and Janet, the wiry dyke, were dating now and she looked to Kyle for advice. Mostly, Kyle just listened for the few minutes she could spare. DJ and her new lover were both smitten and doing fine.

Joe paced, then finally came over and gave Kyle the evil eye. Kyle held out the order in one hand and the phone in the other, indicating that DJ was on a roll that was impossible to interrupt. Joe made obscene gestures until Kyle hung up.

Five minutes after DJ, Lyndi phoned—thankfully on Kyle's cell—to ask her out for Saturday night. Very interesting—they usually "dated" only on country night and left the rest of the week to other lovers that fate provided. She must be missing Kyle after the LA dyke interrupted their routine. Kyle accepted the date after a proper amount of stalling, then went dutifully back to the window display.

Luckily, her first lesson wasn't for an hour. She could assemble two new drum sets and get them into the window by then, and worry about the window signs later. Meanwhile, she could indulge herself in Lyndi fantasies, her favorite. She had the drums out of their cartons, and was sorting out the hardware on the floor, when her cell rang again. *Jesus!* She was going to let it go, but Allie rarely called her.

"Hey, Allie. What's up?"

There was an uncomfortable pause. "Kyle, a baby dyke in my youth group committed suicide last night."

"Oh, God. I'm sorry, Al. How old was she?"

"Seventeen."

"Geez, what happened?"

"Her neighbor saw her outside the Center, holding hands with her girlfriend. Told her parents."

"Oh, no." Kyle got the picture.

"They went ballistic—enrolled her in some fucked-up Christian boot camp in Colorado. Last night, she called her girlfriend to say goodnight, didn't mention *anything* about suicide, then took a bunch of her mother's pills. Nobody knew until morning. The friggin' morning they were taking her away..."

"Damn."

"Listen, the big thing now is the other kids. They're in shock. Really messed up. To top it off, the family is having a closed funeral."

Kyle said, "You mean no queers."

"Right." Allie paused. "Kyle? If you could help..."

"*Me*? What can I do, Al?"

"Come to the memorial tomorrow night at the Center, on Fourth Avenue, across from Delectables. All the kids will be there. Christina's coming, and I'm gonna call DJ and Judi and Raz."

"Al, thanks but I...I wouldn't know what to say."

"You don't have to say anything. Just be there. A warm, queer, strong, adult body just being there."

"I don't get it, Al."

"See, what if you're a kid and your friend dies, and it seems like nobody cares? What if you're devastated and super pissed? Some of them, like Sandy, aren't even out yet. There's no adult outside the Center to talk to. So, we have to honor Sandy's life and deal with our loss—together, as a community. We have to do *something*."

"Got it. I'll definitely come, Al. What time?"

"Seven. Thanks, Kyle.

"See you tomorrow, Al," she replied gently, feeling the depth of Allie's grief. "Take care."

- 22 -

Melissa Ethridge's classic, *Keep It Precious,* filled the big meeting room at the LGBTQ Youth Center. The usual motley furniture, plus thirty or forty folding chairs, faced a simple table in front. A single, unlit white candle was placed there, surrounded by pictures of Sandy with her friends that some of the kids had brought.

When Kyle and DJ came in, Christina waved to them, and they hugged her, and then took the seats she had saved for them. The place was packed, yet the room was subdued. Members of the youth group sat in a circle on the floor in front of the table. Twenty or so teens were talking intently with Allie and the other organizers. Kyle suddenly recognized Mystery Woman among them. At the sight of her, Kyle's stomach took its usual elevator ride to her throat.

DJ saw the woman at the same time and whispered, "Is that her?"

Kyle nodded, nervously.

"I'll ask Chris..."

Kyle whispered, "Great, but later. It's starting..."

The music was ending, and a young dyke from the youth group stood up near the table. She self-consciously lit the single candle to open the memorial. There was an immense silence as she found her scribbled notes in her pocket, looked at the crowd, then stuffed the papers back into her pocket. Her soft voice wavered, "My name is Marcia. That was Sandy's favorite song. She was my best friend and...my girlfriend. We're here tonight to remember her and...and say good-bye."

Unable to continue, she sat down cross-legged on the floor, and put her head in her hands. The two teens on either side put their arms around her.

Without missing a beat, Mystery Woman stood up. "I'll go next. My name is Angie."

Angie. Kyle missed her first words in the thrill of knowing her name. *Angie.* Kyle could study her now, being invisible in the audience. A mixture of fear and desire rose in her chest. She was holding her breath. She forced herself to breathe and listen.

Angie was saying, "I used to call Sandy *Supergirl* because she was so amazing and I knew she could do anything. When she was scared, I'd push her to go for it—for college, for a scholarship, for a girlfriend...It was our thing."

DJ nudged her arm and Kyle looked over. She mouthed the words *Christina knows her.*

Kyle elbowed her to be quiet, secretly thrilled at the news.

Lovers

Angie continued, "One day last year, I was bitching about how there's almost no legal help for the women I see at the shelter. *If I were a lawyer, blah, blah* and Sandy nailed me. It was her turn to push. You know the rest. I applied to law school and just got into NYU."

Applause broke out, especially from the kids in front.

Angie's voice broke, "I'll never be able to tell her now." Then, with conviction, she continued, "I knew Sandy would be fine when she got away to college. This was her last year here, with parents who couldn't appreciate the beauty, the extreme beauty and bright future of their own child. She didn't make it to that future. But, she's coming with me, for sure. I'll never forget her. We'll all take her with us, wherever we go."

By now, some of the crowd was crying. Others brooded in their anger.

A skinny, six-foot-something, shaved-headed boy stood up next, then waited a moment, awed by the size of the crowd. He sported six or eight earrings and other jewelry, red lipstick, black undershirt ripped open to reveal a ringed nipple. Under his short kilt, a line of tattoos ran down his left leg, disappearing into a high black boot.

"I'm David and I'm pissed. Sandy didn't kill herself. Her parents and their church killed her."

Everyone in the crowd took in a single, horrified breath. Then, a vocal wave of angry agreement swept through the room.

"I'm out and proud…" he his outfit, pausing for applause, "…to show her hateful parents and assholes like them that we're not afraid. We're not gonna hide…" More people broke in with applause.

"We're not gonna change…and we're not buying your

stupid camps and shrinks and sermons. It's all just hate and ignorance."

By now, the whole youth group and some adults were standing.

"You'll never kill us all." David put his fist in the air and a torrent of applause and angry noise followed. All of the youth in front stood with their fists in the air, then all but one sat down.

A chubby, femmy girl, barely fifteen, remained standing. "I'm Allison. I still can't believe Sandy's...dead. It's like she's gonna show up late—any minute—like she used to. If you can hear me Sandy, we love you a lot...We miss you."

Andy, one of the adult mentors, stood up to add, "I'm Andy and I feel the same thing, like where's Sandy tonight? There's a big hole in the group. I wish I could thank her—because it shows me how much each of you means to me. So, I'm telling you here, every one of you, I love you. It's crazy how I've gained you, somehow, in a deeper, realer way, from losing her..."

A young lesbian and gay boy got up together, not at all softened by Andy's words. "Me and Garrett and Sandy were best friends—since sixth grade! Oh, yeah, I'm Melanie. Her parents won't talk to us—except her father said, 'Don't come over. And stay away from the funeral.'"

Garrett took over. "They won't tell us when it is. Or anything. But, we're her real family and we've gotta be there for her."

A ripple of agreement went through the group.

"So when anyone finds out, let us know. We'll tweet the location. We're gonna crash it, and I hope everyone will come."

There was a wave of applause and agreement as the two sat down.

Allie stood up. She hadn't the faintest idea what she was going to say. She looked out at the crowd and down at the kids. A wave of love, infinitely tender and compassionate, rose from her heart into her throat. Everyone waited. This was no time to get choked up.

She started talking. "You guys are right. Hate is insane and it kills whatever's beautiful. This time it took Sandy. But are we gonna hate back? You know, hate the haters? Can you *hear* that? It's crazy just saying it, right?"

A murmur of assent went through the crowd. Allie was on a roll. "So you chill and look for justice. Well, there's no justice to find in this. Sandy lived with hate. She's free of it now. She made her own decision. Any one of us would reverse it now if we could. But we can't. So we grieve her tonight, together. Our deep feelings unite us and make us more powerful than before."

Something like hope or expectancy quietly took over the room.

"Now what are we gonna do about it?" Allie paused for a moment. Then hit by a flash of inspiration, she continued, "I say let's party!"

A man in the audience blurted out, "*WHAT?!*"

Everyone roared with laughter and the energy broke. Everybody talked at once.

"What are you talkin' about, Allie?"

"You go, Allie!"

Allie relaxed and continued. "Yeah, I mean it. Like David said, we're not gonna hide. And it's stupid to hate back. And fuck the funeral. Sandy's not gonna be there anyway. So, yeah, let's have a huge party—in Sandy's honor. I guarantee she'll come to that!"

Huge applause!

A straight-looking middle-aged man stood up. "Yeah, it could be a fund-raiser for the youth group. I know a lot of parents from P-FLAG who'll come to *that* party."

The applause kept building.

A sweet looking cowboy stood up. "The Rodeo Association is behind it a hundred percent."

A lesbian in a business suit stood up. "And the Queer Business Association."

Then, a gay couple, "And the AIDS Coalition."

Everyone stood up now and cheered their brains out, even those who were crying.

And that's how Sandy's memorial ended and her party began.

If you asked Allie what happened there, she'd tell you she was making it up as she went along. If you got her really serious or really drunk, she might share her actual experience: Totally at a loss, she felt suddenly connected to Spirit, connected to everyone, feeling the divergent streams of group energy, accepting them all, allowing them to merge into one current inside, wrapping it into words and sending it back out, and knowing that everyone is being perfectly taken care of, even Sandy, and always has been, and always will be, and feeling so much love and joy she wanted to laugh and cry and embrace everyone at the same time.

She'd tell you that after an hour or two, the connection faded. By now, she knew the high of unity would return, but she never knew when. Sometimes it came out of the blue, like tonight. More predictably, it came in meditation, or in the height of passion, wrapped in Christina's arms.

- 23 -

"I never knew you were such a party dog, Allie," said Kevin, putting his arm around her. "We'd be proud to call you a fag."

Everybody at the table gave Allie a round of applause—Kevin and his lover, Ed, Christina, Kyle, Angie and the Amazon, and maybe five or six more lesbians and gay men. Needing to stay together after the memorial, they had gone to the Greenery for coffee. It was like a family gathering and Kyle felt conspicuously new. She hardly knew Christina, DJ had gone to work, and Allie was preoccupied with everyone else.

But, the main thing was that Kyle was self-conscious, uptight, and turned on, sitting almost across from Angie.

Whenever Kyle looked at her, the Amazon sitting by her side caught Kyle's gaze instead. It wasn't exactly friendly. More like locking eyes with a driver's license photo, or St. Peter on a bad day at heaven's gate.

Allie raised her cup and everyone did the same. "To Sandy's party. May it be the best ever!"

"To the party!" everyone answered.

"Listen," Angie said, "Even if we use the Center, we'll need the whole parking lot..."

"Yeah, it'll be a big turnout," said one of the men.

Allie picked up on the idea. "Lots of lights outside. And food..."

"And a stage. Music and dancing," Angie spun out the thought.

"DJ can host," Allie added.

"Maybe we'll need the street, too…" Kevin mused.

"I'll ask Theresa if her band will play," said the Amazon.

Kyle barely heard anything being said. Angie's voice still echoed *music and dancing* in her mind. When Angie spoke, Kyle's gaze lingered on her and got lost. Right now, she studied Angie's profile, her high cheekbones, the two simple gold loops in her earlobe. Kyle imagined her lips brushing past the cold gold to kiss Angie's neck and shoulders.

Somewhere in the distance, Ed asked, "Do Micky and Gary still have a band?"

"I'll call Gary," one of the other men replied.

Allie said, "Maybe Kyle will play, too. Huh, Kyle?"

The sound of her name brought Kyle back to the group. Angie turned toward Kyle and smiled. Not just Angie, but everyone was looking at her, awaiting a reply. "Uh," said Kyle, embarrassed, "I don't have a band, Al."

Christina jumped in, "We know lots of musicians, not just bands. Let's do a jam next week, so people can sort out who they want to play with. Kyle can play—and everybody else—and no worries, you know?"

"I'll do it, then, for sure," Kyle said, wondering where that came from.

"Great! When should we party, guys?" Allie asked.

Ed said, "Well, we need time to organize, letters with donation envelopes, articles in the papers, maybe a permit for the street...

"So, six or eight weeks," Kevin finished his sentence.

"Right, four or five weeks," said Allie. "Otherwise, everyone will forget what it's about!"

Everyone laughed. That was Allie. And no one doubted that the party would happen sooner rather than later.

Allie continued, "Anybody want to meet Saturday with me and Kevin and Angie and the kids to organize this thing?"

Ed waved his hand over his head, "I'm up to here..." Kevin shot him a look. "But, I'll set up with the kids the day of the event—tables, stage, equipment..."

"It'll all come together," said Allie, suddenly tired. "We'll organize everything Saturday, one o'clock. Everybody who wants to come, come. All the kids will be there."

Kevin said, "There it is. What do you say, Edwin?"

"Yeah, I'm beat," Ed replied, getting up. He left two twenties on the table to cover everyone. "Goodnight everybody."

The group broke up. Angie and the Amazon said goodnight to friends at their end of the table. Kyle thanked Ed and waited for Allie and Christina. She was too shy to approach Angie, especially with the Amazon at her side. Standing aloof, Kyle

Lovers

was content, knowing she would see Angie again.

Suddenly Christina was next to her, calling to Angie, "Hey, Ange! Miriam! Wait a minute. Let me introduce you guys so you know each other next time."

She introduced Kyle to Angie and the Amazon, whose name Kyle instantly forgot. The feeling of Angie's hand in hers rendered everything else a blur.

Out in the parking lot, Allie grabbed Kyle as she headed for the truck and took her aside.

"Kyle, listen. Christina just had a brainstorm," Allie whispered excitedly.

"Lay it on me, Al,"

"You need a roommate for Mexico, right?"

"Uh...right."

"You know who could share your room?

"Who?"

"Why don't you ask Angie?"

"*WHAT? Me?* I don't even *know* the woman, Allie!"

"Okay. Right. You just met her. That would be weird..."

"And her girlfriend would throw a fit."

"What girlfriend?"

"I can't remember her name. The Amazon."

"Miriam?"

"Over there. She's leaving with her right now."

"That's her roommate. They've been friends since kindergarten. So, what if I ask Angie? She's really great. We could all talk more about the benefit..."

- 24 -

Six thirty-six a.m. Allie checked her watch as she paced Kyle's living room. She was super excited about Mexico and wanted to get going. Plus, she couldn't stand being late for anything. Christina was waiting in the car. They still had to pick up Angie, get gas, and meet the other car at the freeway in twenty...two minutes. Kyle shouted something unintelligible from the back bedroom.

Allie yelled, "WHAT?"

"ALLIE, COME IN, GODDAMMIT. I'M NOT GONNA KEEP YELLING!"

Giving up, Allie went to the bedroom door and looked in. "Oh Jesus, not this..."

Kyle's almost-packed bag was on the bed, along with her

entire wardrobe. Shorts and shirts were strewn everywhere. Rat lay in the middle of it all, watching the show.

Kyle asked, "Do I look stupid in this?"

Her tone of voice triggered Allie's compassion. She knew exactly where Kyle was at. "No, it looks great," said Allie, sincerely.

Kyle took off the sleeveless t-shirt anyway and put on a regular t-shirt. "How's this?" she said, checking herself in the mirror.

"Excellent," Allie replied.

Kyle started pulling the shirt out of her khaki shorts, stopped, and tucked it back in. "Do I look like a suburban housewife or something?" she said, glowering into the mirror.

"Totally, and I look like Carrie Underwood," Allie laughed. She gave in to the moment, moved some shirts aside, and sat down on the bed. "What's makin' you crazy, Kyle?"

"How'd I get talked into this?" Kyle complained. She took off the khaki shorts and picked up a pair of black jeans.

"Forget it," said Allie, to save time. "*That* looks stupid. It's 105 degrees..."

Kyle went on, "I can't believe I'm sharing a room with a woman I don't even know."

"She's great, Kyle. Believe me. *We* know her."

"Oh, *that* helps."

"You've got the whole ride down with me and Christina to get to know her."

Kyle put on a pair of cutoffs and frowned into the mirror. "Allie, do you know how awkward this is? Do you like these pants?"

"The tan ones were better. I know it's awkward."

Kyle put on the khaki shorts again, and looked in the mirror.

She knew this was as good as it would get. "I give up," she said, defeated. It was the only way a fashion crisis ever ends.

Allie said, "She thinks you're cute."

"She does? How do you know?" said Kyle, expectantly.

"She told me last night."

"Last *night!* Well, thanks for telling me."

"DJ told Christina you like her, but you didn't say anything to me, so I was kind of, you know..."

"Terrific," Kyle said cynically. "If Angie and I ever get together, I'll be the last one to know."

"You got a hat?" Allie asked.

Kyle started fooling with her hair. "Why? Is my hair that bad?"

"For the beach, duh!" Allie laughed.

Kyle threw a cap into her duffel. "You guys didn't tell her I'm crushed out or anything, did you?"

"Nope," said Allie. "Not a word. Are you?"

"Nope," said Kyle, impenetrably. "I just think she's cute."

Kyle picked up Rat and rubbed her face all over Rat's head. Rat squinted and hung there like a sack of laundry. "Bye, my big watchcat! I left you lots of food."

As soon as Kyle put her down, Rat raced out of the room, having better things to do than say good-bye.

Kyle grabbed her bag and scanned the room for anything forgotten. "Okay, I guess I'm ready," she said, resigned.

Allie said, "Hey, take your time."

"Butthead!"

- 25 -

Allie relaxed as soon as they hit the almost-deserted highway, almost on schedule. The second car, with Raz, Judi, Erin and Patty, followed close at a steady seventy-five. Allie loved driving, loved her fast little Prius, loved Christina and her friends. For her, everything was as full of promise as the open road across the desert, the new sun in the sky. They would be at the beach in Rocky Point by two. Plenty of time for a swim and a nap before dinner.

Leaning against the passenger door, Christina broke out an endless stream of sweet coffee from a big thermos. Angie brought a bag of pastries. Christina kept the coffee and conversation circulating into the back seat, and fed bites of pastry to Allie as she drove.

Kyle, being Kyle, had a bout of intense, self-generated fight-or-flight before she finally settled down. She was hyper-aware of Angie just across the back seat. Angie's legs were shaved and smooth, in honor of the beach. Baggy tan shorts, small scar on her calf, serious running shoes. Black tank top. Kyle watched the muscles in Angie's arm as she raised her coffee to full, waiting lips. *Does she work out? Maybe racquetball or tennis.* A line of wet coffee on Angie's upper lip glistened in the sunlight until Angie licked it off. *Am I staring? Am I being ridiculous?* Her senses overloaded, Kyle turned away and looked out her window at the vast desert—for way too long.

Kyle knew that, right now, overcharged with excitement, she could have a laughing fit, lose her voice, spill coffee, or drop anything she touched. So, she had herself reeled in pretty tight. She leaned into the back door and retreated into her corner, doing exactly the opposite of what her body urged her to do. It was so extreme that Angie asked her twice if she had enough room.

Just being attracted to someone had never messed Kyle up like this. Lust had been her loyal friend, especially for the last two years. Whatever it was with Angie, it wasn't just lust, although there was plenty of that, too. Kyle was more powerfully drawn to—and simultaneously more afraid of—this beautiful woman than anyone she had ever met. Including Jessie. She had no idea why.

"That's Kitt Peak Observatory up there, Kyle," Christina said. "Great place to see the universe. Maybe we'll go there on a tour some night."

"Cool." Maybe it was obvious from Kyle's tone that although she was looking out the window, she was seeing nothing.

Angie leaned over and pointed out Kyle's window, calmly, steadily, so Kyle could follow her finger to a little white dot on the distant mountain.

"That's it," Angie said, very close to her ear.

Kyle turned and smiled automatically. She looked into Angie's dark eyes for just a moment, until the fear took over. Angie was close enough to kiss, and the closeness took Kyle's breath away. Involuntarily, Kyle shifted her body even farther away from Angie. Too close. Too fast. Angie moved back to her side of the car.

Christina kept talking and somehow, as Allie had predicted, Kyle began to relax. She was getting used to being near Angie now, and loved it, despite her fear. It felt like a thousand watts going through a hundred watt bulb. Maybe she was adapting to the charge. It was starting to feel very good.

Allie cranked the music and settled in for the long haul. The others talked for a while, then looked out their own windows or played with their phones. Soon, Christina and Angie slept. Kyle closed her eyes, but couldn't keep them closed. She had to keep checking to see that it was all real. Okay. Good music. Desert passing by. Allie driving. Christina and Angie, sleeping. Angie, so near! So awesomely, sensually, uncomfortably near!

Kyle took in the curve of her back, her hair falling over her shoulder, her soft skin, soft breathing. Without waking, Angie took a deep breath, shifted a little, and turned her face toward Kyle. *Oh my God, what a glorious woman!* Her breathing resumed its soft, slow rhythm and Kyle watched her, enthralled. When Kyle finally looked away, she saw Allie smiling at her in the rear view mirror. Kyle grinned, leaned forward, and put her hand on Allie's shoulder.

She said quietly, "Hey, Al, you good driving?"

Allie replied, "Couldn't be better. The road's mine and we're right on time. Great view, huh?"

"Best ever," Kyle laughed. She rubbed Allie's shoulders a while, then settled back. Somehow, she fell asleep.

- 26 -

After a few hours, and just before the turnoff to Mexico, Allie pulled into a roadside ramada for a picnic lunch, with Raz right behind her. The women wolfed down a potluck lunch for eight—everything from fried chicken to empanadas, strawberries, crackers and cheese. Kyle wondered if she would ever have strawberries again without thinking of Lyndi. But, the thought was very short-lived.

With a renewed obsession to hit the beach, both cars switched drivers, filled up at the last gas before the border, and continued south. Christina slowed to thirty as they approached the first tiny town in Mexico. Soon, she kept it at twenty, ready to encounter kids, dogs, farm animals, working people, tractors, bicycles, you name it on the road. A few locals checked them out as they passed by.

As if reading Kyle's mind, Christina said, "They see *everybody* come through here, Kyle. We're no big thing. It's the only road."

Kyle loved the wood and stucco buildings with chipping pastel paint. The ancient railroad station. The tiny corner market and one-pump gas station. One or two modern buildings—perfectly groomed houses with lush gardens next to shacks in total disrepair. Side yards with goats and chickens. Front yards with clotheslines and kids and shrines to the virgin. Old cars everywhere.

It took little more than a minute to pass through the entire town. Christina picked up speed and slowed again only for the few, isolated towns along the way. They talked about women and life and, when they got tired of that, they cranked up the music and sang. Finally, about ten miles away from the beach, bigger and bigger houses appeared along the road, then shops, and then a traffic light, which they hadn't seen for hours. The unmistakable, salty smell of the ocean filled the air.

Soon they were checking into a clean-looking, little motel overlooking the beach, actually four small buildings around a little courtyard and bar. They got their own building with four double rooms, thanks to Allie and Christina's good planning. Luckily, Kyle and Angie got the room at the end, next to Raz and Judi. They wouldn't have to listen to Allie and Christina making love...

Kyle opened the door into a sparse and clean little room with two twin beds, a small table and two chairs. She stood aside so Angie could enter first, more out of awkwardness than butch gentility. She had never been alone with Angie before.

Angie scanned the room, apparently pleased, and nodded at

the beds. "Do you care?" she asked.

"Nope," said Kyle, as casually as possible.

"Me neither," said Angie, tossing her overnight bag on the farthest bed and flopping down after it. "Hmm, pretty comfortable," she said, bouncing a little.

Kyle noticed the springs were quiet. *God, can't I think about anything else?* She headed back out, having forgotten her bag.

"How's your room?" asked Allie, unloading the car.

"Great. As long as I never go there."

"Get in there," Allie laughed, thrusting the duffel bag at her. "Swim in ten minutes, okay?"

Kyle strode back into the room, just as Angie pulled up her bikini top over bare breasts and shoulders. Both felt the shock of sudden intimacy.

"Hey," said Angie to Kyle, who had stopped in her tracks. "This is a little weird, isn't it? We hardly know each other."

"Yeah," Kyle said, awed by her unapologetic honesty. "I can come back later."

Angie started to laugh. "I usually don't care too much about privacy. Did you see me jump when you came in?"

Kyle lied, "No," and added, "But, it did feel like walking into the girl's locker room for the first time in seventh grade..."

"Oh God, raging hormones and total embarrassment!" laughed Angie.

"That's about it." Kyle finally laughed, blushing.

"I'll keep that in mind," Angie said, grabbing her towel and throwing it over her shoulder.

Kyle thought of a hundred funny things to say after Angie closed the door behind her, leaving Kyle to change.

"How are you two doing?" pried Allie, who waited for them

outside their room. The others had already left for the beach.

"She's unique," said Angie.

"Is that good or bad?" asked Allie, but Angie only shrugged her shoulders and smiled.

"Race you both to the beach," said Kyle, bolting out the door and speeding past them.

"You asshole," Allie took off after her, with Angie right on their heels.

The runners easily caught up to and passed the rest of the group ambling to the beach. They swam. They baked. They napped in the sun, then swam again. Without discussion, Kyle used the bathroom to change for dinner, giving Angie lots of time to get dressed in their little room. Two by two, the group assembled in the courtyard, then walked the few blocks into town. They scored a patio table with a wide-angle view of the sunset and lingering magenta sky. Pleasantly high on margaritas, they feasted on grilled shrimp or the fresh catch of the day.

Kyle loved everything. The sun, the swim, new friends, and some good tequila helped her relax into happy excitement. Great food and conversation distracted everyone from noticing that she was studying Angie, crushed out on Angie, as if there were a bright spotlight on Angie in the beautiful night. Everything else, every wonderful thing, had receded into the background.

As the flan was served for dessert, Kyle's excitement shifted into worry about what to do later, in their little room. *Even at the other end of the table, I can feel her breathing, read her feelings, imagine her hands on me. Allie never said the room would be the size of a postage stamp. Maybe I could pretend to go right to sleep. Not even get undressed. That would look stupid. I can't mess this one up.* And on and on. Allie and Angie both noticed that Kyle had become withdrawn and preoccupied. But, she seemed happy enough, and they chalked it up to the margaritas.

Later, outside the motel, the little group planted their beach chairs in the sand to watch the ocean and the stars. Raz's two friends, Erin and Patty, left early to look for a party. Allie and Christina were next, followed by everyone but Raz and Kyle. The two stayed on and on, accompanied by a friendly bottle of tequila. The night was magic, to be sure, but Kyle was mostly avoiding the little room until Angie was asleep.

- 27 -

After a huge, late breakfast, the pals claimed their share of beach. They created an island of blankets, beach chairs, coolers, and clothes and settled in for a lazy day. It was clear and hot with a light, cool breeze coming off the water. The colorful sails of a dozen catamarans dotted the horizon.

Allie and Kyle were the first in the water, followed by everyone but Christina and Judi. In a heaven of her own making, Christina lay on a Wonder Woman towel, earbuds ensuring her complete exit from the world. In a royal blue bikini and sunglasses, she was a nice complement to the life-sized superhero beneath her. Judi sat nearby in a beach chair, glued to her Kindle, devouring the latest lesbian romance.

One by one, the pals returned from the ocean, slathered on

sunscreen, and chilled out. Allie and Kyle were still in the water, bodysurfing until they dropped. Kyle already looked blue, but she would freeze to death before giving up the ocean to Allie. Angie sat on a blanket with her hands wrapped around her knees, apparently looking out to sea. Behind her shades, she watched Kyle, unobserved.

Angie loved Kyle's lithe, athletic body, so graceful in play—as long as she thought no one was looking. With her short, wet hair slicked back, and her beautiful high cheekbones, Kyle reminded Angie of a teenage boy. But her features were much too fine to be male, and the curves of her Speedo much too feminine. It was hard to type her. Magnetic, yet withdrawn most of the time. Aloof, except with Allie, who brought out her crazy, competitive kid. Was she shy or wild, brooding or just vacant? Whatever it was, watching her was getting Angie very excited.

When Allie and Kyle finally came out of the water, they raced each other to shore. Out of breath and laughing, they fell onto the blankets at the same time.

"I won!" claimed Allie.

"I won!" said Kyle, louder.

"They all saw I won," Allie argued.

Christina said, without moving, "She's such a jock."

Dripping wet, Allie leaned over Christina, winking to Kyle. A stream of cold water hit Christina's bare stomach.

"AAGH! Stupid!" Christina yelled, throwing Allie a towel and a warning look.

Immediately, she lay back in place and closed her eyes. Having grown up with six kids in the family, she was impervious to almost any intrusion. Nothing could move her against her will except a real emergency. Allie lay down next to Christina, this time careful not to get her wet.

Kyle was too full of energy to just lay there all afternoon. Gathering her courage, she asked, "Anybody wanna go for a walk?"

Raz, Judi and the rest, already into their books and music, grunted negative. Unexpectedly, Angie said, "I'll come. There's no telling who you'll pick up otherwise."

"Ooh!" said Judi and Christina, simultaneously, at the low blow. Christina sat up on one elbow.

"Don't do me any favors," Kyle said, taking her on.

"I wasn't calling you a slut, Kyle. I don't know you that well," said Angie, getting her shirt. Game on!

"Ooh!" said Judi and Christina on cue.

Angie went on, "Seriously, the men here will hassle anything female that's alone and still breathing."

"Well, then, I accept your generous offer of protection," said Kyle, rubbing some sunscreen on her face and arms.

Angie put out her hand for the sunscreen. "I've got your back."

Judi put her book down and shot a look at Raz, as Angie's long fingers more-than-thoroughly sunscreened Kyle's back and shoulders. Raz winked at Allie and Christina who were also enjoying the whole thing. Kyle closed her eyes so no one could see her getting completely turned on. She returned the favor for Angie.

"Later, you guys," said Kyle, as nonchalantly as possible, as they headed off.

"Later," echoed Angie.

Even Christina sat up. Everyone shamelessly watched Kyle and Angie walk away. They were gorgeous together, and any lesbian could sense the chemistry between them.

Angie said, "You feel all those eyes glued to your back?"

"How about a long, passionate kiss?" joked Kyle. "That'll give 'em somethin' to talk about..."

"Maybe later," Angie said, and ran off down the beach.

Kyle took that as a possible *yes*, boosting her confidence and her already happy mood. Angie ran and Kyle chased her until the pals faded into the distance behind them.

They took a long walk at the water's edge, their bare feet caressed by the waves. Their hands seemed to come together, magnetically, to physically connect them. But, both women worked hard to keep them apart. Two toddlers stopped them to admire their rudimentary sand castle. The little girl offered Angie her shovel to add a bucketful of sand, and she happily obliged. Farther down the beach, two hunky college boys launching a catamaran invited Kyle and Angie aboard. Clueless that the women were lesbians, they tried English first, then Spanish. The women smiled and acted as if they didn't understand, and the young men watched them walk away, laughing.

Angie and Kyle spoke little. Yet, they were the center of their own, private world. Nothing was in focus except themselves and their bodies, freely exploring the seemingly endless beach. Out of the blue, Kyle said, "That was cool, what you said at Sandy's memorial—how she pushed you to go to law school."

"You remember that? It was true. Sometimes your friends take you more seriously than you do."

"You working at the women's shelter until you go?"

"You *remember* all this? Yeah, I love it. I've been there three years. I never thought I'd get into law school. Then, BAM—NYU! That one *Dear Ms. Robles* is gonna totally change my life."

"How come New York?"

"Stanford—Rejected. UCLA—Accepted but no money. Michigan—Accepted but no money. Then, NYU offers me a full scholarship, housing, expenses..."

"Sounds like fate."

"I'm on the waiting list at U of A."

"So you can still get in?"

"Yeah. If someone they accepted takes a better offer, I'm in."

"Geez, what would you do?"

"I don't know. In-state tuition is almost nothing. My family—in every sense of the word—is here..."

They both fell silent to watch a tiny girl with an ice cream cone walk by in total ecstasy, holding her mother's hand. She had wall-to-wall chocolate smeared from her chin to her nose, dripping off her hand, and brown patches all over her bare chest. A newly dropped chunk was melting onto her sandal and her foot.

"Reminds me of me," laughed Kyle.

Angie laughed, and then asked, "What about you?"

"I look good in food, too," Kyle deflected, trying to leave it as just a joke.

Angie persisted, "All I know from Allie is you're a musician, swapping houses with a friend. What's the deal?"

"My friend, Liz, has a summer project back home at UC San Diego. She's in grad school here at U of A in Social Psych."

Angie said nothing so Kyle would go on.

"And I'm teaching keyboard and minding the store at Music City. That's all there is."

"Come on."

"Okay. Okay. I played in a band. Hated my day job. Needed a break. Liz calls with this crazy idea of a house swap. So I did it."

"That takes guts. Is it working out?"

"Sure. I like Tucson. I wasn't expecting anything, so... It's like life. Maybe you find out what it means by the end."

"This *is* life—I hate to tell you."

"Right. Thanks a lot. I might have missed that." Kyle turned to follow a woman passerby. "Awesome legs..."

Angie had noted the woman, too. "Mmm. You miss San Diego? Your friends?"

"Mostly my best friend, Nandi. I wrote a song last week and I want her to sing it. She's amazing..."

"You guys ever record?"

"Nah. Maybe someday—I don't know. If I keep writing, and it's good enough..."

Angie became suddenly animated, raising her voice, "If...if. No man would ever say that. Women are taught from this high—she indicated a toddler's height—to doubt their own voice, their own worth. It drives me crazy!"

"Geez, no mercy!"

"Life is short. This is life..."

"Okay, okay. Maybe it's naive, but I thought coming here for the summer would break me out of my rut. Help me see my life—or maybe lack of it, as you so *tactfully* pointed out—more clearly.

"I think you will."

"Will what?

"Do something amazing."

"Why? You don't even know me! You've never heard a friggin' note!"

"No, but my instincts are good..."

They walked back to the pals, saying little, comfortable in their own thoughts. Kyle wondered why this woman believed in her, for no good reason. Talked to her so honestly and intimately. Called her on her shit. And got her so insanely hot at the same time.

- 28 -

Sunday night of the 4th of July weekend—a traditional time for tourists and locals to go out of their minds, with one more day to recover before going back to work. Starry and warm, it was the pals' last night in Mexico. After a late dinner, Erin and Patty followed the live music ramping up in the courtyard bar. Judi and Raz relaxed outside the motel with Raz's bottle of tequila, watching the moonlit beach below.

Kyle and Angie walked the beach with Allie and Christina, their senses wide open to the light breeze and the waves rippling over their feet. Unconsciously, they filled themselves with ocean sounds and smells so they would always remember, and could always come back in their minds. The four women walked separately, not holding hands, but sometimes touching.

Each was conscious of the unspoken rule against lesbian "sex" in public. So, they were cautious, even though they had the beach mostly to themselves, with just a few other couples and an occasional runner. On their way home, they stopped at the water's edge, watching the waves meet the stars.

Sprawled in their lawn chairs at the motel, Raz and Judi passed the bottle of tequila and watched the foursome on the beach below. With a little imagination, it was better than TV. Just without the sound.

"You think they're gonna do it?" Judi ventured. "I bet they do. Whataya think?"

Raz snapped back, "Who's gonna do what?"

"Now, who is right in front of your face?" said Judi, copping an attitude. "I'm not asking for telepathy here, just a simple connection."

Raz replied, "Well, why can't you just say it? I mean I could actually be thinking about something else."

"Not likely, Mz. Sagittarius. I say you were thinking what I was thinking," said Judi.

Raz would not give in. "I say, assume psychic autonomy at all times. And if you wanna dish about Kyle and..."

Judi said, "See! I knew you knew! You just wanna argue."

"You are impossible! Knew what?" said Raz, exasperated.

On the beach, a horny heterosexual couple had stopped very close to Allie for a long, long kiss. They groped and groaned without a thought for anyone else. Allie cleared her throat, and then manufactured an over-the-top coughing fit until they moved on, hand in hand.

"You won that one," laughed Kyle, thinking that Allie was trying to be funny.

"I hate that," Allie said vehemently, glaring after the couple.

Christina replied, "Yeah, I don't care if they're straight. But, why do they have to flaunt it in public?"

"I'm serious," Allie said. "Don't you ever wish we could kiss—or even hold hands—here? I mean without worrying about getting killed?"

Christina moved toward Allie seductively, "Kiss me right now, Macho Girl. C'mon, let's risk it."

To her credit, Allie did not look around, paranoid, even though she had every reason to. Being a triple minority, she had encountered her share of ignorance. Whether it was the ocean or the moonlight or being with her friends, she momentarily forgot about bigots, rabid fundamentalists and all the rest. She took Christina into her arms and kissed her passionately, seriously, momentously. It was the right thing, the only thing, to do. Emerging from the kiss, she looked deeply into Christina's eyes, then flashed a wonderful smile.

"I love you!"

"Alright!" Christina said, "Baby's first kiss in public."

"It's history, Allie," said Kyle, happy for her friend.

"And a much better kiss than the Gropers," said Angie.

"I love you guys," laughed Allie, "Now, let's go home." She took Christina's hand without thinking and headed up the path toward the motel. Kyle and Angie followed them, both wondering whether to take the other's hand.

- 29 -

Millions of random thoughts raced through Kyle's mind as she took a shower. Nothing coherent. Gerbil-on-a-wheel thoughts. Another late night with tequila and Raz? No, thanks! It's time. I have to do something. She's different. This is different. I'm a mess. How can I...

She cranked the water as hot as she could stand it, to help her mellow out. To dry herself, Kyle had to crack open the bathroom door to let out the steam. Either that or die. The fog was thick. Drops of water were running down the mirror. She threw on a clean muscle shirt and boxers, then tried to dry off the mirror with her wet towel.

Angie appeared at the open door in just her tank top and underwear. "Hey, it's a sweat lodge. Let me get my drum!"

She threw the door open to air out the bathroom and joined Kyle at the sink.

"Well, come on in. Plenty of room," said Kyle, facetiously, noting Angie's takeover of the bathroom. Kyle watched her load up her toothbrush with an esoteric, organic herbal toothpaste. "How can you brush your teeth with that stuff?"

She took out her own twisted, travel-size Crest.

"What are you talkin' about?" Angie held up her tube of toothpaste. "This miracle product, here?"

"It's pigeon shit. I almost died from it."

Without thinking, Kyle grabbed Angie's toothpaste and gloated, "I'm gonna throw this out and save your life."

Angie grabbed for the toothpaste, but Kyle was too quick. She gave Kyle an almost-threatening, trying-to-be-serious look, and put out her hand.

"Give it back," she demanded.

Kyle replied by forcefully squeezing a huge blob of toothpaste into Angie's open hand. In a single, swift motion, Angie rubbed the whole mess across Kyle's face.

"Aaaaah! That does it!" Kyle screamed.

She chased Angie into the bedroom, stopping momentarily to squeeze out a giant blob of the stuff into her right hand, ready for Angie's face. They faced off, smirking at each other, one on each bed.

Angie yelled, "NO!"

Kyle yelled, "YES!"

"NO!"

"YES!"

Kyle chased Angie from bed to bed and finally grabbed her, both of them laughing and out of breath. Kyle slimed Angie's face and neck with the white goo. Angie grabbed for the tube.

They fell to their knees, wrestling over it.

"Gimme that!" demanded Angie, grabbing at Kyle's clutched hands.

"Hah. Try to get it!"

Angie tickled Kyle. Totally unprepared, Kyle screamed and dropped the toothpaste.

Angie and Kyle both pounced on it. "Let go!" demanded Kyle, but Angie had it.

"Give it back!" Kyle said louder, still struggling.

"No way!" laughed Angie.

"Shhh!" said Kyle. She pointed with her chin to the wall and the pals next door, just trying to distract Angie. Angie didn't bite, although she was now conscious of the racket they were making. Kyle grabbed for the toothpaste. It didn't work.

Angie whispered loudly, "Cut it out! It's my toothpaste!"

"Okay, but I don't trust you," Kyle whispered back.

"Okay, truce," whispered Angie.

They both laughed at their own stupidity. Whispering was ridiculous!

"Can I trust you?"

"You don't trust me?" Kyle laughed. "I'm the one wearing most of it! See?" Kyle rubbed a sizeable glob of toothpaste off her face, then held out her hand as proof. Looking around, she now had nowhere to wipe her hand. She looked mischievously at Angie.

"NO!" Angie shook her head. "Truce, okay? Really truce."

Unexpectedly, she took Kyle's hand, full of toothpaste, and rubbed it across the bottom of her own shirt, ending the fight. "There. Truce."

Kyle thrilled at the curve of Angie's body under her hand.

"Your shirt..." Kyle stammered.

"No worries. Wait..." Angie reached out to wipe the rest of the toothpaste off Kyle's face. Kyle backed away, still mistrustful.

"Easy. Easy. Come on," Angie said in a low, sweet voice that melted Kyle's defenses.

Kyle sat still, not quite trusting, but surrendering anyway. She closed her eyes. Angie was miraculously close. Angie rubbed the last streak of white off Kyle's face with the bottom of her shirt. Then she ran her hand across Kyle's cheek, and kissed her lightly on the mouth.

"That's better," said Angie, letting her hand move across Kyle's throat and neck. Kyle gasped. She opened her eyes and looked at Angie with unmasked expectancy and desire.

"That is better," Kyle said, just above a whisper.

Angie looked deep into Kyle's eyes, totally accepting. Wanting her. Kyle leaned forward and kissed her again lightly. She touched Angie's face and ran her fingers around her slightly open lips. Then, because the closeness was so intense, she kissed her cheek and her neck before returning to her mouth. Kyle kissed Angie more deeply this time, and it crossed her mind that she could still back away.

Instead, she searched Angie's eyes and suggested, "Let's lose that wet shirt."

Angie nodded. Kyle expertly took the shirt over Angie's head. Half naked now, Angie smiled slightly and found her desire mirrored in Kyle's eyes. She ran her hands through Kyle's wet hair, then across her face, neck, and breasts. Kyle held her gaze and, somewhat out of character, let herself be— explored. Inside, every cell was on fire under Angie's touch.

"Angie," Kyle whispered.

She pulled Angie close and kissed her passionately, pressing

Angie's breasts hard against her. After the long kiss, Angie took a deep breath and leaned back. Gently, exquisitely, Kyle traced her breasts with her hands, looking into her eyes, then kissing her neck.

When Angie got up to light a candle, Kyle took off her own shirt and leaned back on the bed. She was wet, her boxers were slick, and her body burned with desire. Something deeper was there also, an urgent longing for Angie to touch her, know her. Even now, just beginning, this was the most intimate lovemaking she had ever experienced.

Angie's face was now illumined with candlelight. She was beautiful beyond this world. The flickering light played on her body as she came to Kyle. Gracefully, she slipped out of her underwear, lay over Kyle, breast to breast, and kissed her deeply. Kyle sighed and melted, tracing Angie's spine with her open hands as they kissed. She shifted slightly to her side, to trace Angie's breasts, circle her nipples, and draw a line down her torso. She moved her hand between Angie's legs. Angie groaned. She was as wet as Kyle.

Kyle traced the wetness around her clit and Angie kissed her with abandon. Then, wanting more, Angie sat up and straddled Kyle, taking Kyle's fingers deep inside her. Both women moved rhythmically as Kyle's thumb circled Angie's clit, first lightly and then with increasing pressure. Angie moved to take Kyle's fingers deeper. Kyle circled her nipples with her tongue, and very lightly bit the hard centers, then licked them. Angie responded with a groan and tensed her pelvic muscles again and again around Kyle's fingers. Kyle watched her, touched her, loved her completely. Angie, in her passion, was the most beautiful thing she had ever seen.

At the end, Angie looked into Kyle's eyes with unmasked

love and desire, then closed her eyes again to be in her body, to *be* her body climaxing in Kyle's hands.

"Oh...Ohhh...Mmm...Ohhhhhh..." When Angie came, she leaned back and came intensely, fiercely, finally pushing against Kyle's hands to stop. Then, sighing, she lay forward on top of Kyle, with Kyle's fingers still inside her, heart to heart, fitting perfectly together, as the last waves of orgasm rippled and finally stopped.

Kyle felt like half of a miracle. She kissed Angie's face and played with her hair, slightly moved her fingers inside her just once, and then was still. Angie rested a few moments, and then let out a deep sigh of contentment.

When Kyle took her hand away, Angie turned on her side and stretched out next to Kyle, resting her hand on Kyle's chest, her knee across Kyle's legs. "Listen," she whispered in Kyle's ear, "You can hear the waves from here."

They lay entwined and listened. The sound of distant waves and the rise and fall of their own breath was almost more intimate than lovemaking. No one had ever looked that deeply into Kyle, or allowed Kyle to know her so openly. Now they lay together as if they had done so for a thousand years.

Angie began to stroke Kyle's breasts lightly. Then she kissed her neck at the same time, then behind her ear. Kyle wanted to kiss her hard, but forced herself to be patient. Angie moved her kisses to Kyle's breasts, taking them in her mouth, then licking the nipples hard. She stopped to pull off Kyle's boxers, and then came back to her mouth for a deep kiss. Her tongue filled Kyle with an intense urgency. Angie knew it would, but she took just a little more time. She wanted Kyle as much as Kyle wanted her. But this was their first time. And the first time happens only once.

- 30 -

Tuesday night after Mexico, Kyle was home alone after fantasizing about Angie all day at work. She felt totally pumped all day, but couldn't concentrate, and so accomplished nothing. Now, she narrowed her possibilities to drinking at the bar (and thinking about Angie) or calling Nandi (and talking about Angie). She called Nandi.

Spinning her memories of Angie into a story, Kyle told Nandi about the weekend, from the scary ride to Mexico to the heavenly ride back, all over each other in the back seat. "I really like her, Nan. It's not just lust."

Nandi laughed. "*Not Just Lust*. I love it! Perfect title for your memoirs. You seeing her tonight?"

"Nah. Too early to call."

"You're joking. Too early for *what*?"

"Too early to high dive into no water."

"Hmm, she scared you. And now you're playing games."

"C'mon, Nan. There's no future in it. She goes to New York in August and I'm coming back to you, my true love."

"What happened to right now, tonight?"

"Be here now? I did that and got burned, remember?"

"That was different."

"Look, I'm in too deep already. I miss her after one friggin' day!"

"You like her. Duh. That's how it works."

"Okay, so we could have a few weeks in love and a lifetime to get over it."

"That's a totally twisted way to look at it."

"Thanks."

"You better call her."

"I *am* gonna call her," Kyle said. "I'm just waiting until at least tomorrow. Anyway, the phone works both ways."

"Yeah, I know. Just have a heart if you can, Kyle. She's probably going through the same thing."

That hadn't occurred to Kyle. And what did she mean by *have a heart if you can?*

"Okay, you're right. But listen, Nan, the other reason I called you was I uh, I volunteered you to perform at a benefit concert with me."

"*WHAT?* Are you outa your mind? Where?"

"Here."

"You asshole!"

"It's a benefit for the LGBTQ youth group."

"You're kidding, right?"

"Uh…no." Kyle told her the whole story about the

memorial and the party.

"Asshole! When is it?

"Middle of August. It's perfect timing. I send you a plane ticket. You come. We sing. Stay a few days. Then drive back to San Diego together. Brilliant, no?"

"Hmm. What's the deal? Is Mz. Angelina involved?"

"*Angela.* Yes, she's involved. But, so are all my friends. I really want to do it with you, Nan. It's gonna be a great concert. I mean, don't you *miss* the music? It'll be phenomenal. You've got to come."

"I'll think about it."

"Don't! Just come!"

- 31 -

Seven-thirty on Friday night. Kyle waited nervously in Angie's living room, holding a bouquet of flowers behind her back. Miriam, the Amazon, had let her in, said almost nothing, and disappeared into the kitchen.

Angie had called on Wednesday night to arrange the date, leaving a message on Kyle's answering machine. That night, Kyle was fucking her brains out with Lyndi as usual. Kyle remembered the look of disbelief on DJ's face when they left the bar together after dance class. For DJ, it didn't compute, after hearing Kyle rave about Angie and Mexico. For Kyle, Lyndi just happened—again—and she let it.

Luckily, Allie had gone home right after class. With any luck, Angie didn't know about Lyndi. But what if she did?

Kyle had made no promises. Why should she? For some reason, though, here in Angie's living room, she felt guilty. She was totally self-conscious about the flowers. Too corny? Too little too late?

She studied the photos on the mantelpiece, especially the one of Angie with her parents and the one of her with Allie, Kevin and the youth group. Kyle moved over to the mirror to check her hair. She winced. Angie was standing behind her in the mirror. Lyndi revisited!

"Kyle! You scare so easily."

Kyle looked into Angie's eyes in the mirror and responded too theatrically, "I'm not scared. I'd forgotten how beautiful you are."

"Oh, that was *good*. Totally fake, but good. You brought flowers, too."

Kyle turned around and gave the flowers to Angie. "Yeah, I'd better tone it down. I'm even scaring myself."

"I like it," Angie said. "The truce must still be on."

Kyle smiled, remembering Mexico and their toothpaste truce. And making love! She felt immediately better—and completely turned on. They leaned together and kissed lightly. Then Angie took her to the kitchen to fix the flowers and meet her roommates—Miriam, and Miriam's lover, Daniela. Kyle sat down at the table with Daniela, and the three talked and joked while Angie found a vase and arranged the flowers. Miriam remained aloof, loading the dishwasher with as much clatter as possible. Either she deeply disliked Kyle or had a stick up her butt, or both.

Kyle and Angie had a leisurely dinner on the patio at Caruso's, an Italian place with a candle on every table and Christmas lights all around. They shared a week's worth of stories about Music City and the women's shelter over Chianti and a very fancy pizza. Money and the bill were already on the table. Pensive and distant, Kyle watched the movement of the candle's flame.

"Did you like the dinner?" asked Angie.

"What? Oh, the pizza. Loved it," said Kyle, pointing to a spot of red sauce on her shirt. "I only wear home the very best...Really."

Angie smiled. "What should we do now?"

Kyle looked at her watch. "Wow, almost ten. Too late for a movie. Work day tomorrow..."

Sensing Kyle's emotional exit, Angie tried to bring her back. "I missed you last week."

"Me too. It was kind of a wild week," replied Kyle, deflecting.

"Mexico is a hard act to follow, isn't it?"

"Yeah," said Kyle, offering nothing.

"Would you have ever called me?"

Jesus, she's fearless!

"Of course. I was gonna call you that same night." Kyle hated the lie as soon as she said it. Lying to this woman was too painful...

Only half-believing, Angie searched Kyle's eyes, looking for something real. She wanted to get to know Kyle beyond the distant fantasy of Mexico, and the xxx-rated fantasies she'd been having all week.

Under her gaze, Kyle blurted out, "Aren't you finding this hard at all?"

"Sure," admitted Angie.

"I mean isn't it maddening that on a scale from one night to a lifetime, we have maybe six *weeks*? How weird is that?"

"Nothing with you has been ordinary for me." Angie looked directly into Kyle's eyes, searching.

Angie's confession found a perfect match in Kyle's heart. But, it also created a crossroads in her mind, and Kyle chose the road to nowhere. She responded by averting her eyes and doubling her resistance.

"Well, then how can you act so normal, like *What should we do now?* I mean, I don't have a clue about what to do now, alright?" Reeling herself in, Kyle added, "Maybe we should go."

Letting it drop, Angie got up immediately.

Driving Angie home, Kyle brooded. *What is WRONG with me? Why don't I invite her home where we can be alone? And make love, like I imagined all week. I've never worried about the future before. Okay, that's* another *lie...*

"Sorry, Ange. I'm just tired. And I have to work tomorrow." All that was true.

Angie didn't reply. She knew it was all bullshit, but had decided not to challenge her. She couldn't read Kyle at all.

Kyle rambled on, trying to be funny, "I must be getting old, letting my job interfere with my life. It's always been the other way around."

"How old are you?"

"Twenty-seven."

"Yeah, they say twenty is the new sixty."

They laughed and lightened up. Kyle brushed her hand against Angie's cheek and smiled. It was thrilling to touch her. Angie melted and smiled back, putting her hand on Kyle's thigh. A bolt of desire cut through them both at once. Kyle turned her eyes back to the road. She wanted this woman so badly! But, she didn't dare. *She's a real-life fantasy, but real life doesn't work like fantasies. She's a heartbreak waiting to happen. Don't do it! Don't do it!*

Turned on and conflicted, Kyle drove Angie back home in silence, even with Angie's hand on her shoulder, then her neck, then running her fingers through the back of Kyle's hair...

"Want to come in?" asked Angie, as the truck stopped in front of her house.

"Uh, I'd better go." Even Kyle could hear how mechanical she sounded, but she kept right on going. "Let's go out next week. I'll call you."

Kyle walked Angie to the door. Angie had hoped to see Kyle again over the weekend, to make the most of time. But, Kyle obviously needed time—or something—to deal with their relationship.

Angie said, "See you. Thanks for dinner." She gave Kyle an uninspired kiss goodnight. By now, she was unable to sustain enthusiasm and desire on her own, and frustrated with trying.

As she opened the door, Kyle said, "It was great. I'll call you." And then she added, "Or, you call me." She could have absolutely kicked herself for saying that!

Angie shut the door behind her, not bothering to reply. That last "*or you call me*" put her over the top.

Kyle dragged herself toward the truck. She stopped and looked back at Angie's house. It was bright and inviting—in this moment, the center of her universe. Everything brave and good in her wanted to run back and bang on the door.

But, she didn't.

Inside the house, Angie stormed in on Miriam and Daniela watching TV.

"Aagh!" she screamed.

"What happened?" asked Miriam, ready to kill Kyle if necessary.

Angie ranted, "No heart. Totally gone. Asshole! How'd she lose her heart? In a week!"

Daniela said gently, "I know you can lose your head. I never heard of it the other way."

Kyle was opening the door to the truck when the front door flew open. Fuming, Angie stood in the doorway and yelled, "KYLE!"

Shocked, Kyle looked up and said...nothing.

"Do you want to know me?"

"What?"

Angie just stared at her, with contained fury.

"Is this a trick question?" Kyle tried to make a joke out of it.

"Do you want to get to know me? It's not this hard. Believe me!"

Kyle walked around the truck to the sidewalk. "What do you mean?"

Angie stayed at the door. "I mean—Get real. We've just got the summer, okay? Maybe we'll hate each other in two hours or two days. But, that would be way better than another fucking minute of *Thank you very much.*"

Kyle took a step toward Angie and stopped. She was speechless. No woman had ever been this honest with her. It was totally out of her reach.

Angie continued, "Okay, you're leaving. I'm leaving. So what? Call me when you wake up. No more bullshit!"

Angie flew inside and slammed the door behind her. Her hands were shaking. "I can't believe I did that!" she said to Miriam and Daniela, who stared at her from the couch.

"It's good!" defended Daniela. "You're not taking any

crap."

"There goes a real idiot," growled Miriam. Then, with more compassion, she added, "What *happened* tonight? You had such a great time in Mexico."

"Yeah, but maybe it was just me," Angie answered, dejectedly. Sadness and hurt were creeping in now that her anger was dissipating. "I *think* she felt it, too. Now, she's so...cold."

"Or she's just a player..." said Miriam, cynically.

"One minute she acts like the love of your life. Then, pfft. Gone!" Angie tapped her temple. "Worry, worry, worry..."

"Enough!" Daniela pronounced, leaping up off the couch. "Mirie, c'mon. We're taking Angie to the bar. That mindfuck shit is contagious!"

"What?" laughed Angie. "You're not even gonna listen to my sob story?"

"You need to dance it off, girlfriend. Have a drink. Maybe get a little female attention. Sexual healing. Who knows? C'mon, let's go!"

"Wait a minute, guys..." said Miriam, as Daniela sprang into action. "We're right at the end of the movie!"

Daniela shot her a look and disappeared into the bathroom. Miriam got up and checked her hair in the mirror, knowing she was right.

"This is crazy!" Angie protested.

"No, this is Friday, Ange," philosophized Miriam, "We're not gonna let it go to waste."

- 32 -

10:30 Friday night. Prime cruising time.
 DJ pumped up the music into a sensual rush. Kyle chugged a beer and watched the dance floor dejectedly while DJ worked. In spurts, she told DJ the whole sorry-ass story of her date with Angie.
 "That *is* lame!" DJ said. "You gonna call her? Go on. Call her now!"
 Kyle drained the last of the beer. "What am I gonna say?"
 "I'm a novice, okay, but how 'bout *I'm sorry*?"
 Kyle said nothing. So, of course, DJ continued, "Or maybe read something from Wikipedia or the history of Scotland …anything, really."
 Kyle stared into space.

Lovers

"Or, how about sharing a recipe for trout?"

"I hate *processing!*"

"You're right. It's worse than death. But you know you should call her. Maybe admit you're an idiot. That always works for me."

"Nah, I'll call tomorrow—apologize and start over or, actually, continue over." She laughed. Her beer was kicking in. She welcomed the mindless ignorance that would come with the next one.

Waiting at the bar to order, Kyle felt a hand sweep across her jeans and pat her butt. Kyle turned and Lyndi flashed her brilliant smile.

"I'll have whatever you're havin', lover."

Kyle lit up. "Lyndi! You look amazing!" Alcohol greatly exaggerated her delight at seeing Lyndi—sexy, uncomplicated Lyndi.

Moving up in line, Kyle yelled to the bartender, "Two lights!"

Kyle paid for the drinks, clinked bottles with Lyndi, and took a long swig of beer. With her arm around Lyndi's waist, she stared into the crowd, seeing nothing.

"Hey, where are you?" Lyndi asked, flirtatiously.

"Huh?"

"You're brooding. Wanna dance? It'll cheer you up."

"Sure, why not?"

Kyle gave herself over to the music and her sexy lover, now boldly seducing her. She forgot everything but Lyndi. Angie, tomorrow, all her fears, everything faded far into the background. Focused only on Lyndi, Kyle was hot and excited, yet strangely at peace.

At one point, DJ finessed the juncture between songs so

insanely that most of the women dancing instinctively looked up toward the DJ's booth, including Kyle. DJ was staring at Kyle and mouthing exaggerated, undecipherable, words, which Kyle found extremely funny.

Still dancing, Kyle laughed and yelled to DJ, "WHAT??"

DJ repeated whatever it was, and Kyle laughed harder.

DJ tried again, "ANGIE—IS—HERE."

Finally understanding, but not believing DJ's joke, Kyle shook her head, "No, she isn't."

Determinedly, DJ repeated slowly, "YES—SHE—IS!"

Lyndi shot Kyle a questioning look, and Kyle responded, "DJ's just jerking my chain."

Lyndi spun around and ignored them. When Kyle turned back to give DJ the finger, DJ was pointing her own finger—toward the bar, deadly serious.

Awareness finally dawning, Kyle turned with dread in that direction, her stomach turning inside out. "NO," she closed her eyes. "Oh, no."

She saw Angie, Miriam, and Daniela at the bar, talking intently. At least none of them was looking at Kyle.

"Let's get outa here," Daniela was saying to Angie.

"No. It's her problem, not mine."

"Fuckin' idiot," Miriam offered. "I'm gonna go talk to her."

"No!" said Angie, putting a hand on Miriam's arm.

Kyle stopped dancing and yelled to Lyndi, over the music, "I've gotta go."

Lyndi yelled, "What's wrong?"

"Sorry. Someone's here. I've gotta go."

"Okay. Later." Unconcerned, Lyndi moved over to dance with a couple she knew. She would never, ever ever be lonely.

Angie and her friends watched Kyle and Lyndi talking on

the dance floor.

Miriam said, "I think she saw you, Ange."

Angie looked down at her drink, collecting her feelings.

"Here she comes," announced Miriam. "What an asshole!" she added, when Kyle was within earshot.

Kyle approached the group, totally distraught. Miriam and Daniela turned toward each other and ignored her.

"Angie," Kyle shouted over the music. "Angie, can you come outside and talk?"

Angie turned to her friends, "I'll be back." She threw an icy glance at Kyle. "Come on."

Kyle followed Angie outside. Two young dykes were enthusiastically making out near the door. Angie walked just beyond them and stopped, folding her arms.

Kyle said, "Look, I'm sorry. There was no way I could sleep."

"Hey, if you want to be with her..."

"C'mon, Ange. I just met her here."

"I'm not blind, Kyle."

"I mean, you know, I ran into her."

Irritated by the women making out and the lack of privacy, Kyle replied, "Dammit, this is too crazy. Please come home with me so we can talk. I live just two blocks away."

"I'm with my friends, now."

"Listen, I'm sorry. I didn't ditch you to come here. I should have come in. I should have called right away after Mexico. But...uh..."

Angie just glared at her, not helping at all.

At a loss, Kyle stared at the sidewalk, then said quietly, "I'm sorry. Can we go somewhere and talk? Anywhere..."

Angie was still cold. Kyle could be such an idiot.

"Please come over. I'm sorry. I'm stupid." The beer was at least helping Kyle be candid. "Ask them to drop you off later, okay?"

Angie just looked at her. Kyle was at least trying...

"I'll text you the address," Kyle said desperately, grasping at hope.

"You are somethin' else!"

"I'll wait up for you!"

Angie turned and headed back into the bar.

"Angie, please. Say *something*..."

The door closed behind her. Ashamed, Kyle did not follow.

At home, Kyle paced the living room. She waited with frantic expectancy, then with growing despair. The shock of seeing Angie at the bar kept flashing through her mind. Each time she winced with self-hatred. PTSD! But, unwilling to give up hope, she sprawled out on the couch to wait, all night if necessary. Rat jumped onto her lap and they dozed.

The doorbell jolted them both awake. Rat flew off Kyle's lap and ran for the kitchen. Kyle raced to the door, her heart beating wildly.

"Angie!" she cried, flinging open the door.

Angie waved to her friends. Miriam left rubber as she sped off.

"You came!" said Kyle, meeting Angie's eyes with amazement.

She kissed Angie passionately, innocently, like a long lost love returning home. It was exactly what Angie wanted, what she had wanted all week. She felt the rightness of it, despite Miriam's warnings. But, when she again sought Kyle's eyes, they were steeled for apologies and recriminations.

"Angie," Kyle began, "I wasn't…uh…"

Angie interrupted, "We'll figure it out later, okay?"

Kyle's heart melted. She felt immensely guilty, relieved, and forgiven, all at once. She burned for Angie, but an aching tenderness spilled out instead. She kissed Angie softly, sweetly. Angie returned the kiss deeply, tracing her fingernails down Kyle's back, wanting passion, not gratitude. Kyle's body immediately understood.

- 33 -

Ecstatically useless at work the next day, Kyle phoned Angie four or five times. Because it was a busy Saturday, Joe needed her and felt abandoned. His mood disintegrated from paternal to tolerant to cranky to maniacal. Kyle knew he couldn't help it. But neither could she.

Kyle bee-lined home as soon as she got off work. She and Angie made dinner together, and then alternated talking and making love into the night. Kyle told her about loving Jessie and hitting bottom afterward, about her life in San Diego, and even the hypercritical, unsupportive family that she never saw and didn't miss. Angie talked about her ex-lovers and Miriam and her big, close-knit family.

Lying in each other's arms, they lamented having only a

short time to be together. At least both were leaving Tucson. No one would be abandoned, and no one blamed. Missing each other would be far better than missing what might have been. So, they made an uneasy truce with time. They saw each other every day. And they never talked about it again.

- 34 -

Friday came again, way too fast. Angie had spent a hellish day in court waiting to testify for a woman from the shelter. Afterward, starving, she picked up a pizza and went straight to Kyle's house rather than home. She had a key now and let herself in. She yelled hi to Kyle, but no response, just the sound of the shower. Kyle wasn't expecting her for another hour.

She grabbed Kyle's cap off of its hook in the hallway, put it on backwards, and headed down the hallway, "Pizza Dude! Anybody home?"

Kyle called from the shower. "C'mon in. Come in with me."

Angie threw open the shower curtain with one hand, holding

the pizza in the other. "It's Pizza Dude! Are you the lady of the house?"

"Not exactly," laughed Kyle, water streaming over her naked body.

Angie put down the pizza and started taking off her clothes. "Pizza Dude is smitten. She should just leave the pizza and go back to work, but…"

Kyle jumped on board. "Wait a minute. It's more than that. Maybe this woman orders pizza every night. She's obsessed. But the Dude uh, never delivers what she really wants...

Angie looked at Kyle playfully as she undressed. "Yeah, Dude wants her bad. But she's too shy. Silent type..."

Kyle went on. "So the woman leaves the front door unlocked and gets into the shower, *knowing* the Dude will show up, and hoping...

Kyle held out her dripping hand. Naked, Angie took it and got into the shower. She gasped as Kyle wrapped her wet self around her, kissing her hello.

"Oh, they needed that," Kyle said, stepping aside so Angie could get fully under the shower. She ran her hands down Angie's back and around her waist. Angie sighed as the water rushed over her face and hair. It was an exquisite feeling, together with Kyle's touch. From behind, Kyle cupped Angie's breasts in her hands, and whispered in her ear, "I've been waiting for you..."

Angie lost track of the story. Kyle was kissing her neck. Her hands were already on Angie's stomach, then tracing her thighs, then between her legs. Angie put one leg up on the edge of the tub. Kyle stroked her with both hands, and held her open to the play of the water.

Kyle pressed her breasts against Angie's back and said

softly, "The woman couldn't help herself. She had waited so long..."

The water flowing over her, Angie moved to take Kyle deeper inside. Kyle followed her, increasing her pressure with both hands, not letting her get away.

"Ohh," sighed Angie, breathing hard.

"You feel so good," whispered Kyle, staying with her, firmly, evenly, until Angie came with a vengeance.

Afterward, Angie leaned back against her and relaxed. "God," she said, still breathing hard. Kyle pressed her body into Angie, breasts to back, feeling Angie's breath rise and fall much faster than her own.

When Angie turned to kiss her, Kyle whispered, "The woman wondered if it was Dude's first time..."

"Dude actually gets around, " smiled Angie. "She's been crushed out a few times. But, she's never really loved. Or been loved in return."

"I see," said Kyle. "What is it this time?"

"We'll find out," said Angie playfully.

They dried off, trying to kiss at the same time. The story melted away, and it was just them, naked and still aroused. Angie led Kyle to the bedroom and they lay down on the fresh cool, sheets.

Heaven!

Angie bent over Kyle and kissed her deeply. After the kiss, Kyle looked up at her, smiling, leaving her lips slightly open, running her hands down Angie's legs. Angie kissed her again, fervently, and then again, wanting more. Then, she kissed Kyle's breasts and stomach, gently pushing her legs apart. She covered Kyle's thighs with kisses, then ran her tongue around Kyle's inner lips and took her clit into her mouth. Kyle moaned and arched her back. Angie opened Kyle with her tongue and moved it inside of her, then across her clit, then back inside in a beautiful rhythm, loving the taste of her and the beautiful intimacy.

Kyle lifted her hips and opened herself to Angie more and more until she came, making a long, moaning sound from some ancient part of her. She shook involuntarily, legs trembling. Soon, Angie realized Kyle was crying. Worried, she moved quickly to lie with Kyle. But when she saw her face, she knew Kyle was fine. She was actually radiant, natural, like a child, in total release. Angie put her arms around Kyle, her knee between Kyle's legs. Kyle wrapped herself around her lover and cried, more gently now.

Angie held her and said, "Okay. It's okay."

"Sorry," Kyle gasped, "Never happened...Wow!"

"It's okay," Angie said. "It's beautiful. A deep…release…of feelings…"

Angie felt no separation between the woman in her arms and herself. Her chest felt open, and Kyle's heart was beating there. Kyle's taste lingered on her lips, her tears on Angie's face, their bodies entwined. Kyle was quiet now, breathing softly along with Angie. For the first time, Angie felt her lover at peace.

They woke up together, needing to move, needing to pee, needing to eat. Night had fallen around them and their skin was cold wherever they weren't touching. For a moment before getting up, they looked into each other's eyes. Protected by the twilight, they searched for confirmation in each other. Still unshielded, a powerful stream of love flowed between them, and they shared a last kiss before separating. Then, Kyle made some foolish joke and they laughed and disentangled themselves.

"Where did that pizza end up?" asked Angie, emerging from the bedroom, "I'm starving!"

"And where is my sweetest, most excellent Rat?" Kyle asked, as Ratty showed up right on time for dinner.

- 35 -

The next afternoon, Angie came home from the youth group to find a thin letter from the University of Arizona Law School in the mail. A thrill went up her spine. Even without opening it, it felt like good news—and big trouble.

She ripped open the envelope. *Dear Angela: Blah blah you have been accepted for the fall quarter...*She stopped reading. Her heart pounded. She had totally prepared for New York. She had quietly and painfully untied her heart from her family, the shelter, the youth group, Tucson...*At this time you may apply for a student loan. After your first semester, you may apply for a scholarship and/or stipend...*

Dazed, she went into the house, threw the rest of her mail on the table, and anxiously reread the letter. An explosion of competing thoughts flew through her mind. She had already cashed NYU's first check for travel expenses. Of all nights, she was taking Kyle to her family's restaurant for the first time. She flashed on her address for graduate housing—something Eighty-second Street, New York City. Maybe she should tell her parents about UA tomorrow—or never...

Miriam came out from the back bedroom. "Hey, Ange! When did you come in?" Seeing Angie's face, she added, "What happened? Are you alright?"

Angie shook her head, and her eyes filled with tears. "I can't believe it."

"Is it Kyle?"

"No, we're okay. Here." Angie held out the letter.

Miriam went wild. "Angie! Thank God! Congratulations!" Then, more quietly, "Aren't you happy?"

"What am I gonna do?"

"You're gonna..." Miriam stopped herself from saying what *she* wanted. "You're gonna have two great choices, not just one. And when the time comes, you'll *know* what to do. Right now, just celebrate! God, you just got into the University of friggin' Arizona Law School, grrl!"

Angie recovered and broke into a smile. "I got in. Dammit. I got in!"

She leapt up and grabbed Miriam into a hug. They jumped around the living room like little kids, screaming. After letting it sink in, Angie called her parents. If her family found out from someone else...Well, she could never do that. And if she waited until tonight, the busiest night at the restaurant, her mother would go berserk on the spot.

Angie asked both parents to get on the phone. As calmly as possible, she told them U of A had accepted her, but there was no scholarship, and it didn't mean she was going. There was a long bout of crying and thanking God. Angie repeated the fact that *she* would have to decide. Apparently they didn't hear it the second time either. She listened patiently as they praised her and God for answering their prayers. She was glad she called right away, so they'd have the whole afternoon to get over it.

She waited to tell Kyle in person, when she picked up Angie for dinner. Kyle was genuinely happy for her. As Angie had hoped, the ride to the restaurant gave Kyle enough time to brace for the inevitable parent circus, but not enough time to brood and worry. They promised to talk about it later.

At the restaurant, a waiter welcomed them warmly and led them to a reserved table for two, set with five champagne glasses. On the way, Angie greeted friends of the family at several nearby tables. She smiled, but winced inside, when they all congratulated her. Her parents had obviously spread the news all afternoon, and many of the family's friends and relatives were there to celebrate with them. Angie shrugged it off, realizing she could celebrate the acceptance with them tonight, and still reserve the decision for later. If that turned out to be awkward, well so be it. She would enjoy tonight.

"What a great place!" exclaimed Kyle, oblivious to Angie's turmoil. The restaurant was casual, homey, and beautifully decorated with Mexican rugs and wall hangings. A roving guitarist played for a couple near the window. Every table in the main dining room was full, and soon there would be a line at the door. "I bet they wanted you to join the business."

"Yeah. Lucky for me, my big sister Sonia did. That's her over there." Angie nodded to a striking young woman at the serving counter, talking with the cooks. "Thanks to her, they also gave up trying to marry me off. She's got a husband and a son."

"Jackpot!" said Kyle.

Angie pointed to the bartender, a tall, reserved, handsome man with gray hair, and continued, "That's my father. He hasn't seen us…"

Kyle was noting the resemblance when suddenly the kitchen door flew open. A short, sturdy Latina charged toward them with open arms. Angie said under her breath, "Brace yourself. Here she comes..."

Angie stood up to hug her mother and the woman happily exclaimed, "Angie, my baby! My big lawyer! And your friend, Kate. Welcome! Oh, Angie…"

"Thanks, Ma. This is *Kyle*. Kyle, my mother."

Kyle took her hand and said, "Happy to meet you, Mrs. Robles."

"Yes, it's a happy day for all of us," she beamed. She yelled across the room, "Sonia, the toast! Get your father!"

Angie's father brought two bottles of champagne seated elegantly in a metal cooler. Sonia followed, signaling to the wait staff to pass out champagne and flutes to the other tables. *My god! The whole restaurant is in on the celebration!*

Angie said, "You guys!"

"Congratulations, Angel," said Angie's father, kissing her cheek. "We're so happy for you."

As her father opened the champagne, Angie's mother effused, "Thank god you're not going away."

Sonia shot her mother a look of death.

Angie protested, "Ma, I told you I got *in*. That doesn't mean I'm *going*."

"Well, why not? Isn't this what we've all been praying for?"

Lovers

Sonia took her mother's arm. "Ma, not now..."

But, Angie's mother looked at her knowingly. Suckered into it, Angie replied firmly, "Ma. I told you. NYU's paying my way. I've got to think about it."

"We want to help you, Angel," said her father, pouring the champagne.

"Dad. Please. We'll talk later, okay?"

"Maybe you have other reasons to stay. Not just your family. Isn't that right, Kate?"

"Ma!" Sonia raised her voice.

Kyle blushed.

Deflecting, Angie said, "Dad, Sonia, this is *Kyle*. She's *visiting* from *San Diego* for the summer."

They nodded. Now *everyone* was embarrassed.

Meanwhile, the wait staff had served champagne to every table in the room. Angie's father clinked his glass with a knife to get everyone's attention. He beamed, "To my Angela! Who just got into U of A Law School. We're so proud of you!"

Crying, her mother repeated, "To our Angel!"

Everyone in the restaurant toasted Angie, then burst into a round of applause.

"Thank you, everybody!" Angie stood up and graciously acknowledged the well-wishers around her. Then, raising her glass with a special look to her sister, "And thanks to the most wonderful family in the world. I love you!"

After Angie's toast, Sonia and her father hurried back to work, while Angie's mother lingered to dab her running mascara with Angie's napkin. A waiter soon arrived with a monstrous tray of food.

"Here, Albert," gestured Angie's mother, making room for too many plates.

Kyle blurted out, "Oh, my god!"

Helping Albert serve the food, Angie's mother said humbly, "It's not much, Kate. Take some for tomorrow."

As she left, Angie's mother motioned to the guitarist to come to their table. Kyle and Angie looked at each other and burst out laughing. They finished off the champagne, ate like pigs, and enjoyed dessert with family friends at the next table.

On the ride home to Kyle's, they joked about how sweet and crazy the evening had been. Table by table, Angie described everyone there for Kyle—her aunts and uncles, cousins, godparents, neighbors, people from church, even one of her favorite elementary school teachers. Mercifully, Miriam and Daniela had previous plans or they would have been there, too!

Getting ready for bed, Angie felt immensely grateful to be surrounded by so much love. But, she might still disappoint them all and go to NYU. Although her gut rejoiced at U of A's acceptance letter, Angie's head needed time to catch up. She was still in shock. Was she truly happy about U of A? Or was she just relieved about *not* competing with geniuses at number six ranked NYU, versus U of A at number forty? Or, maybe she was afraid to leave home. Afraid to be alone in New York City. Or a thousand other fears. And who in their right mind would turn down $160,000 in scholarship money? Meanwhile, there was Kyle...Her heart involuntarily leapt with joy. Yes! They would have a chance now...

"Kyle?" Angie whispered excitedly as she slipped into bed.

"Mmm...Yeah?" Kyle answered heavily, already drifting into sleep.

"Sorry about my mother. She's impossible."

Kyle laughed, and leaned up on one elbow. "You mean unstoppable...or maybe relentless. Reminds me of *someone*..."

Lovers

Angie kicked her playfully under the sheets.

"Ow!" Kyle continued, "Really, she's great. And I love the name Kate."

Turning serious, Angie said, "Kyle, I have to decide soon. Can we talk about U of A—and maybe staying in Tucson?"

"Tomorrow, okay?"

"Okay." Angie agreed, but with an undertone of resignation in her voice. She wanted Kyle to be as excited as she was. Couldn't she see that both of them could stay in Tucson now, just as easily as both of them could leave? That the U of A had just offered to rewrite their love story—if they let it.

Feeling Angie's disappointment, Kyle added, "It's wonderful, Ange. But, don't let them push you. It's your life."

"Right," said Angie evenly, feeling suddenly alone.

- 36 -

Way before dawn, Kyle tossed and turned, and couldn't get back to sleep. The uneasy feeling she took to bed now surfaced with an added tinge of despair. Kyle felt conflicted, sad, and angry, as if she'd been betrayed. But, that was ridiculous. Angie had set this whole U of A thing in motion long before Kyle had even met her. Kyle had no clue why she was reacting so badly to such good news.

She watched Angie sleeping peacefully, the slightest smile on her lips. She was so fine. Smart. Strong. Beautiful. *When she comes to her senses, I know she'll leave me, one way or the other.* Angie was so much...better...than Kyle. In every way out of her league. Hell, Kyle didn't even have a league. She was the perfect material for a summer affair. Messed up.

Unattached. In transit. No real job. No foreseeable future. *And then there's Angie, worrying about too many acceptances to law school! Jesus!*

Kyle got up without waking Angie. The ever-watchful Rat was at her heels in a moment, rubbing against her legs as she made coffee.

"You are my good little Rat," said Kyle tenderly to the one constant in her life. "Wanna come sit with me?"

Rat followed Kyle to the living room, jumped onto her lap, and consented to be petted for a few minutes. Kyle felt much better. Checking her phone, she noticed there was a single message from an unknown number in the San Diego area code. *Nandi!*

"Today. One. Twenty. Eight. A.M.," droned Siri's machine voice.

"KYLE!" Nandi yelled, straining over traffic noise. "It's NANDI. At the corner of Thrown Out and Freak Out."

Kyle's heart sank.

A huge truck apparently passed, obscuring Nandi's voice. "...did you really mean, 'Come to Tucson any time?' I'm staying with Liz tonight. Put my stuff in storage tomorrow..."

A techno-voice suddenly cut her off, "Please. Deposit. Two. Dollars and. Thirty-five. Cents...

"Dammit!" yelled Nandi. "I'll call you..."

"Unbelievable," growled Kyle. "Timing is everything, Ratty, and this totally sucks..."

Kyle had coffee ready for Angie when she finally emerged. Kyle waited for half a cup before telling her that Nandi was coming early.

Angie actually laughed. It was that or cry. Her exact words

were, "Now *that's* a sick, sick cosmic joke!"

"No shit. There goes all our privacy and great sex."

"No! I hope not!"

"Kidding. Just kidding! On the good side, I know you'll love Nan. Besides, she was coming anyway for the benefit. Just not for another week..."

After that unfortunate beginning, they segued into the dreaded U of A talk. Kyle's mood downshifted another notch. Sensing her discomfort—with no idea where it was coming from—Angie decided to share everything about U of A versus NYU, but leave their relationship until last. She led with logic, asking Kyle to help her weigh the pros and cons.

First, she praised the great work of the universe on this one—for her, not just her parents. Staying in Tucson would keep Angie's amazing support system intact. At U of A, she could rise to the top of her class, which was not as likely at NYU. She could land a great internship in Arizona, where she eventually wanted to practice, and develop her job prospects and network of colleagues. The best argument for NYU was the full ride. Also, the prestigious program might open bigger and better doors to her future. But, she worried that those national and international opportunities might make her forget the women at the shelter and her real reasons for becoming a lawyer.

Kyle struggled to be upbeat. She had known, from the moment Angie told her about the acceptance letter, that Angie would choose the U of A. Now she understood the reasons why. As Angie described her options with such intelligence and compassion, Kyle asked a few questions, but provided no opinion. She was totally intimidated. Angie was about to enter a world far beyond Kyle's reach.

Angie was glad for the chance to talk this out. By now, she had talked herself into the U of A. Nevertheless, she continued on to her final argument. She was excited that staying in Tucson would put her just an hour plane ride away from San Diego. They could see each other often. Versus coast to coast trips that would be hard if not impossible. Or—of course—they could both stay in Tucson...

Kyle waited for Angie to continue. But, she didn't. She was finding it hard to breathe through Kyle's indifference, hard to be the only one talking. Hard to be the only one who seemed to care. She stopped before revealing how much Kyle meant to her, how much she wanted them both to stay in Tucson, how much she wanted a future together. It was crystal clear that Kyle considered this her decision and hers alone. Angie felt like she'd been talking to herself. Feeling foolish and hurt, she stopped talking.

Angie was deeply offended that Kyle had no opinion about this decision. Why couldn't she say out loud what her body told Angie during lovemaking? Or, maybe she was like that with everyone. Maybe she really didn't care. Maybe for her, this *was* just a summer affair. Maybe she *was* the player Miriam had warned her about...

Finally, Kyle offered, "Well, that's fantastic. It looks like Tucson is winning out. And you'll be close to me."

Angie waited, but there was nothing more. *Close to you? Good luck!* she thought cynically, but said nothing.

Earlier, luxuriating in bed after waking up, Angie imagined that Kyle would persuade her, pursue her, and passionately fight for their future in Tucson. Angie would happily agree, and they would celebrate the new possibility by making love. Or, at least, share their growing feelings for each other and get ecstatic and silly, like she had with Miriam. Instead, all Kyle offered were a few lame and lukewarm remarks, barely beyond congratulations. No champion. Not even an opinion. No feelings. Nothing.

Clearly, Kyle had no heart. Or, maybe, no balls. Either way, did Angie still *want* a laissez faire lover like this? Not in a million years!

So, exactly when the universe made it possible, even easy, to take their relationship to the next level, both Angie and Kyle were pulling away.

- 37 -

Two nights later, Kyle paced the ramp of Tucson's creepy, almost-deserted bus depot. She smiled cynically at the absurdity of it all. She was feeling very sorry for herself as well as Nandi.

A monstrous Greyhound rounded the corner like a beached whale. Splashes of neon reflected on its side. The loudspeaker overhead crackled with static, "The ten fifteen from Yuma is now arriving at Ramp Three. Leaving for El Paso at ten forty-three."

The wide, silver nose pulled in directly in front of her and Kyle jumped back. Even before the driver killed the engine, she could hear frantic barking. It could only mean one thing—Michelle. When the engine went dead, the maddening sound of continuous barking exponentially increased, echoing off the cement walls. The pneumatic door blew open and the bus driver ran down the steps. Nandi staggered out directly after him, juggling her backpack and carry-on, followed by a handful of disoriented passengers.

"Nandi! Hey!" called Kyle.

"Kyle!" cried Nandi, with such relief it melted Kyle's heart. She threw her bags onto the curb and hugged Kyle tight.

"Last stop, you sonofabitch!" said the driver, throwing open the luggage compartment under the bus. He hurled out an oversized dog carrier with Michelle pressed against the bars. Her incessant barking had turned to vicious growling and snarling.

"MICHELLE! Stop!" said Nandi wearily.

"What else?" asked the driver, curtly.

Michelle kept on barking.

"MICHELLE!" snapped Nandi. "For God's sake, it's me, dammit." Then, to the driver, "That green bag is mine, too."

Attending to Nandi's voice, Michelle fell silent at last. Her tail thumped against the side of the carrier.

The driver handed Nandi her duffel bag. "I've been drivin' eight years. And I've heard screaming babies, drunks, dogs, folk singers, cell phone nuts—you name it. But I never heard *anything* howl like that for four hours straight."

Nandi tipped him twenty dollars, an exorbitant amount for her. "Man, I'm sorry," she said, "You've been great. I thought you were gonna dump us in the desert any minute."

"It did cross my mind," he laughed, brightening at the tip. "Hey, you have a good vacation."

At Kyle's, they let Michelle out of her crate in the back yard. Nandi brought her a bowl of food, and then headed for the shower. Rat disappeared as soon as she heard Michelle come through the house. Somehow, Kyle and Nandi would help them get used to each other.

Kyle called Angie. Both admitted they missed each other, but the conversation was light. Angie promised to stay over tomorrow night if Kyle could stifle her moans and groans. They had a satisfying argument about whose orgasms were louder, then said goodnight.

On the surface, everything was good between them. But it had been a rough couple of days. Their brief talk about U of A was behind them, with neither expressing her feelings. Kyle's indifference had wounded Angie deeply. She was too proud to sell herself to a lover. If she had to talk Kyle into staying in Tucson, it wasn't worth it anyway. If Kyle had *any* desire to give the relationship a chance, she wasn't letting on.

Kyle was hurt by Angie's growing coldness. Little by little, she began to steel herself for a break-up. She would keep their beautiful affair going through the summer, just as they had agreed. Then, they could hopefully part on a high note.

Depressed by her brooding thoughts, Kyle turned down Nandi's covers and sat on the edge of the bed, waiting to say goodnight. Today, when she prepared the bedroom, she found Nandi's cowboy hat from their last night in San Diego and put it on the dresser. The hat brought her back to their aborted trip. *What if this were only their second night here, with the summer still ahead? Would she have shared the motel room in Mexico with Nandi? Would she have ever known Angie?*

In sweat pants and a T-shirt, Nandi climbed wearily into bed after her shower.

"Feel better?" asked Kyle.

"Actually, I'm totally trashed."

"I slept for a couple days after I got here."

"I should have come with you..."

"You're here now."

Nandi started to cry. "Kyle, I missed everything. What a waste! I hate myself. But, I hate Jackie more!"

"Listen, I had my turn. Now you'll be the mysterious stranger. The women here will be all over you..."

Nandi took the bait and laughed, "Well, it happens wherever I go..."

They both hugged, grateful for each other to lean on.

Kyle stood up and fixed Nandi's top sheet. "Get some sleep now, Girlfriend."

"Hey, you're tucking me in."

"I missed you, Nan," Kyle said, tenderly. "I'm glad you're here."

Nandi's eyes begin to tear again.

Kyle turned out the light, and called to Nandi from the doorway. "Sweet dreams, Girlfriend."

She closed the door behind her. She knew Nandi, being safe now, would cry all night. The house was empty and dead without Angie. They had spent other nights apart, but Kyle had never felt this sad, this alone. She rattled the box of cat treats and threw a handful across the floor. Rat came out of hiding to chase his treats and reclaim his home. Afterward, Kyle served up his favorite salmon dinner. Rat totally ignored it, leaving to stand guard at the back screen door. He hissed and spit at Michelle, who whined on the other side.

No one was happy.

- 38 -

Kyle arrived at the Midtown Greenery as planned, just as the organizer's meeting for Sandy's benefit was wrapping up. Kyle and Angie hadn't seen each other yesterday and would be apart tonight. So, they were meeting for coffee and dessert—what both considered an anything's-better-than-nothing date. Both had reluctantly adapted to whatever emotional shit was going on. Both were determined to ride it out.

Allie and DJ got up to greet Kyle with a hug. Kyle leaned over to kiss Angie, and then sat down with her friends.

Angie said excitedly, "Tell her the news, Al."

"Your boss, Joe, donated five thousand dollars today."

"God! That's great! Did DJ promise to marry him or

what?"

"No way!" said DJ. "I'm saving myself for the big money."

"Kyle, tell us what's happening with the music," Allie said, in her CEO mode.

"Uh, well, we have some good people on board. We jam twice a week. Nandi came last night and it was amazing. We're still a little rough, but..."

Everybody groaned, knowing how bad *a little rough* can be.

Kyle reassured them, "It's gonna be great. You'll see." DJ added, "Theresa's band and *Severe Tire Damage* are playing sets, too."

"Who the hell is *Severe Tire Damage?*" asked Allie.

"You'll love them," said Kyle. "Trust me."

Allie turned to the teens present, "Never trust anyone who says that!"

DJ asked, "Hey, Kyle. What about backup singers? These stellar youth can sing and dance, juggle basketballs, race gerbils..."

Kyle interrupted, "Backup? Awesome! Yes!"

"*Yes?* You mean it?" said one of the teens, incredulous.

"Absolutely," said Kyle. "I just wrote a song for the closing and you'll be perfect."

"Me, too?" said DJ, suddenly shy when asking about herself.

"Yes! Everyone!" Kyle shot DJ a warm, happy smile. "Come Monday at six-thirty. I'll text everybody my address."

"I'll bring pizza," said Allie.

Angie and Kyle burst out laughing.

"*What?*" said Allie.

"Nothing," said Angie. "Just—nothing. I'll bring a pizza too."

"Pizza is always fun," said Kyle, happy to share their inside joke.

"Okay, it's a wrap. Thanks, everyone," said Allie getting up.

"C'mon, Kyle." Angie grabbed her arm and pulled her to a table as far away as possible. "I miss you."

"Me, too. I thought you might forget me," said Kyle, half-joking, half-resentful.

"Never. You're Kate from uh...where do I know you from?"

After ordering dessert, Angie grabbed Kyle's hand, kissed it, and then rubbed it against her cheek. She needed to touch her for a moment, to feel her presence, beyond the words. She was still hopeful, off and on. At the moment, she was in touch with how much she cared for Kyle. She smiled warmly, "It's good to see you."

"Seems like forever, doesn't it?" Kyle replied. "How *are* you, Ange?"

"Well, I made the big decision. I'm going to U of A."

Kyle took a breath. "That's great. It really is…"

Angie continued, "I canceled NYU today. Sent their money back. Now that it's done, I'm really excited. I can finally be happy with it!"

There was a horrendous pause.

Angie waited. She should have known better. She wasn't trying to start anything.

Kyle admitted, "I'm not sure why I'm having such a hard time, Ange. I really am happy for you..."

"It's okay." Angie smiled, hoping to encourage her. At least Kyle was being honest.

At a loss, Kyle shifted focus onto the present moment, "I wish we could stay together tonight. I feel so...lonely...without you."

"I want to. So much," Angie admitted. "But, it's work."

Kyle snapped, "How can you work 24/7? What about us? You think it's okay to drop the bomb and then just disappear?"

"*Bomb?* I thought it was *good* news," Angie replied, defensively. "I thought you might actually *want* the chance to be closer…"

"I do. I didn't mean that." Kyle grabbed her wallet and left money on the table. If they were going to fight, she didn't want to do it here.

Angie took a deep breath, struggling to re-center herself and hold on to what was important.

Outside in the parking lot, she said, "Remember our first date at Caruso's?" She launched into a great imitation of Kyle. "Uh, don't you think that uh, it's weird that on a scale of one minute to one lifetime, we have maybe six weeks?"

Embarrassed, Kyle replied coldly. "Don't mock me. It was true."

"I know. But, now it's different. We can have more time—if we want."

"I want you tonight," Kyle deflected. "You always put everyone ahead of us…"

Instead of arguing, Angie said softly, "I'll come tomorrow night. Right after work. But, what's this really *about?*"

"It's about your work and the kids and the benefit and all your friends—everything comes before us."

"That will all ease up."

"You think so? We have ten fucking days left and I never see you anymore. Promise me we'll stay together from now on. To make the most of it until..."

Angie interrupted, "Yes. I'd love that. I promise." She

didn't want to hear the rest. It was already clear that Kyle meant to return to San Diego, whether Angie stayed in Tucson or not. Most likely, they would visit each other once or twice. Then, probably, nothing.

Resigned, Angie added, quietly, "I want it too, Kyle." She stopped herself from saying, *probably a lot more than you.*

They kissed, but pulled apart quickly. It felt too much like goodbye.

Kyle walked Angie to her car. Every truce got more difficult. This time, the silence was deafening.

Kyle tried to lighten things up. "How'd you remember that Caruso thing, anyway?"

"It was true. And also very *you*."

"Am I that easy to imitate?"

Angie just smiled at her knowingly, reaching her hands around Kyle's waist, needing to touch her, hold her. She kissed Kyle lightly, sending a welcome thrill through the length of their bodies.

Kyle asked, "Do I always say 'uh'?"

"Only when you're uptight."

They looked at each other and laughed.

"I say it all the time, right?"

"Right."

- 39 -

Kyle's impromptu band, organized for the benefit, was setting up in her living room. They had practiced every Monday and Wednesday night for a few weeks, the only nights their schedules meshed. That officially ended Kyle's Country Night sex with Lyndi. Sometimes Kyle wondered which lucky student had taken her place, now that Angie filled her nights.

This week, they would be practicing with amps, mics for Nandi and Kyle, a full drum set—the works. Predictably, this first setup took forever. The teen backups—Sandy's girlfriend, Marcia, and another girl—hung out with Nandi, Angie and Allie in the kitchen, socializing and devouring pizza and chocolate. Rat played with the cables while DJ and Kyle battled the equipment. The band tuned up. The amps hissed.

The mics hissed. The full setup blew a fuse and killed the lights. Finally, a hideous screech of feedback turned everyone's brain to mush and sent Michelle into a howling fit outside.

Ready at last, Kyle called everyone together and said, "Drum roll, please," and the wild, young drummer, Joanne, produced an ear-bending riff that bounced off the walls.

"Nice! Now that we've got your attention..." laughed Kyle. "We're all gonna learn the closing song, *Goodnight*, the tune that needs backups on the chorus. That would be you guys, Marcia, Melanie, and DJ."

As the teens took mock bows to the band, DJ interrupted, "*Backups*? Oh no, we need a name. How about the Meringues, the Sprouting Jars, the Time of the Month...

Kyle went on, ignoring her. "Here's the chord chart for everybody. First the band will get organized. Nandi and I will sing it through once. And then, we'll work out backup harmonies. Here we go!"

Kyle started the keyboard intro. After a few bars, the band joined in with a steady gospel drumbeat and simple bass. Kyle smiled and nodded. The electric guitar joined in, cautiously at first, and then confidently. Soon, the full band fell into a perfect groove. They were *good*. Nandi took her mic off its stand and began to sing. She started softly, poignantly. At the progression, she kicked up the emotion and the volume. The sound was big and the house was small, and she blew everyone out of the water!

Without thinking, DJ blurted out, "Alright! Yeah!"

Kyle joined Nandi at the first chorus. She sang in perfect harmony, just beneath Nandi's vocal, sharing the same breath.

Allie shot a look to Angie as if to say *did you know they*

were this good? Without thinking, Angie smiled and nodded *yes.* In fact, she looked the least surprised of anyone. Pieces of a puzzle were falling together in her mind. Yes, she knew they were this good, before hearing a note. Her instincts were good, and she had recently been forgetting that.

She knew Kyle. Maybe not the details. But this was her essence, her open heart, here in the music. She knew it would be like this—simple and direct, deep, infinitely loving, infused with spirit. She had seen it in Kyle's eyes, felt it through her emotional armor. Angie listened and watched Kyle intently. She drank her in with her eyes, her ears, her heart. She knew this woman heart to heart, body to body, soul to soul, with a timeless knowing. From now on, she would be able to call it love.

She was in love! She saw Kyle as if for the first time. Her lover. Her beautiful lover!

As Nandi and Kyle sang, Angie watched Kyle intently. She suddenly understood why being in love isn't just attraction. That it's not a feeling, although deep feelings are there. This *knowledge* was love, this knowing the other person beyond knowing. She had never experienced it before. Despite the pressure of time, her own fears, and Miriam's warnings, her knowledge—and love—of Kyle's essence was always there.

Understanding flooded her. *Maybe Love reveals your lover's essence so you can trust. And then, trusting, you can open yourself to her. And, in opening, you yourself can be transformed, like a closed bud opening into a flower.* She had to talk with Allie. What was it like to be in love over time? Working with time rather than against it. Letting time reveal the details about your lover, as she unfolds her essence, and you unfold yours...

Lovers

As the band finished its first run through the whole song, Kyle looked up from the keyboard, catching Angie returning from inner space. She smiled knowingly, and lovingly, because she was returning, too.

As the song ended, everyone cheered and congratulated each other.

Allie marveled, "Liz said you were good. But geez..."

Nandi asked the backups, "Okay, you guys ready to rock?"

DJ looked dejected, *"Clearly,* you don't need us...the nameless backups..."

Kyle insisted, "We *absolutely* need backups."

Nandi added, "We need a whole *choir* of backups. Let's get to work."

Marcia argued, "But we only have three people. And one more practice...

Allie freaked out, *"Ohmygod!* The benefit's on Saturday!"

"Yeah, let's all freak out," DJ suggested.

Everyone screamed, really screamed, and felt better immediately.

Kyle persisted, reassuringly, "You'll be great. All you have to learn is one word—g*oodnight."*

DJ cleared her throat a few times. "Okay, I'm in. All I need is a copy of the words, some iced mocha, throat lozenges, eucalyptus spray..."

"Listen up, backups!" said Nandi, with a firm, yet friendly hand. And everybody listened up. DJ settled down immediately.

Kyle and Nandi still had the gift of *almost* reading each other's minds. It was genius on Nandi's part to step in as the voice of authority for DJ. Kyle just couldn't do it. Together, it was easy to teach the backups their harmonies—joking and laughing as they brought the song to life. The band improvised a bit, then finessed the arrangement during several practice runs. The last run-through was amazing and they all quit while they were ahead. Kyle, Nandi, and the band practiced two more songs, while everyone else hung out.

Angie took Allie aside in the kitchen.

"She'll be gone in a week, Al," lamented Angie. "What am I gonna do?"

"Take it one day at a time" Allie replied.

"I want her to fall in love with me."

"I think she already has."

Angie asked excitedly, "Did she say anything?"

"No. You just seem amazing together." Allie hated to disappoint her. She searched Angie's face. "What about you? You're a gonner, aren't you?"

"Yeah." Tears welled up in Angie's eyes. "It's different for me. She won't talk about it."

"Give her a chance, Ange. You can't blame her for acting like it's a summer affair. It *was* until a week ago."

Angie looked hopeful.

Allie continued, "You hear how they sound. Nandi's pushing her to get the original band back together in San Diego. You and Kyle have got to talk. But, wait for the right time. Everybody's uptight now, before the benefit. And Ange..."

"Yeah?"

"It took Christina two years to fall in love with me."

"No!"

"You know how long it took me? *Two minutes.*"

"Jesus!"

"Hang in there."

− 40 −

The morning of Sandy's party, Joe backed the Music City truck up to the stage, still under construction in the Center parking lot. For the next few hours, Kyle and DJ helped Joe and two sound techs set up mics and speakers, tape down cables, and hook up Joe's giant mixing board out front. Kyle ran inside several times to get Angie, pretending she urgently needed help. Each time, she took Angie to the ladies room for kisses, and the last time more than that. Both returned to work turned on, wet, and distracted.

Ed and two body builders showed up with a truckload of tables and chairs. They set them up along the perimeter of the parking lot, leaving plenty of room for dancing. Miriam's crew hung a hundred strings of white lights everywhere--across the stage, around the parking lot, and throughout the Center. Garrett's crew turned every wall in the Center into a youth art gallery. They asked each artist to set a price for each work, and then doubled it. Half the proceeds would go to the artist and half to the youth group.

Angie's crew set up the big meeting room like a bazaar with tables for information, t-shirts for sale, finger food, desserts, drinks, and a silent auction. All day long, people came with hundreds of pastries and sweets to enter the dessert contest and bake sale. Queer foodies had already volunteered as judges and created categories for themselves, including Best Chocolate, so they could sample their personal favorites. Each chef was asked to set an exorbitant price for his or her masterpiece to donate to the youth group.

Marcia, Melanie, and several other young women set up a smaller room. They hung amazing, poster-sized pictures of Sandy and her friends on every wall. Otherwise, the room was almost bare. The only furniture they included was a simple wooden table and three chairs. At the center of the table, a framed photo of Sandy was surrounded by a vase of yellow roses, a white candle, a big basket, pens and paper, and several boxes of envelopes for donations and pledges. They laughed and cried and sometimes hugged each other as they worked. Although they all agreed to take turns at the table that night, each one believed she wouldn't be able do it. But, later, at the event, every one of them was a mountain of strength, sharing happy stories about Sandy and the youth group, and comforting all that came by.

Allie coordinated the whole effort. She was everywhere, directing and taking care of almost thirty volunteers. Around one o'clock, a nearby restaurant delivered a feast—a fabulous donation in response to Allie's much more modest to-go order. She gathered all the volunteers to eat together, and it turned into a loud and festive party in its own right.

From three-thirty on, Joe did sound checks with the three bands. Wearing his tight, Queen of Music t-shirt and shades, he elegantly directed the musicians from behind the mixing board—and meanwhile tortured the two gay sound techs he had hired for looks rather than ability. By the end, the sound was awesome, and people came from blocks away to check out what was happening. By five-thirty, the night team had arrived and everyone else disappeared to get showers and change. The police showed up right on schedule to cordon off the half block of 4th Avenue outside the parking lot, letting only the food trucks in. By six-thirty, the Center was ready, and the food trucks opened for business.

First, Allie and the pals returned, then a steady stream of youth and foodies. By seven-thirty, as streaks of brilliant pink glowed above the Center, Miriam turned on ten thousand white lights. Overhead, the sky turned royal blue, then deep, deep blue with a million stars mirroring the lights below. The Center was transformed into a wonderland, welcoming at least five hundred partygoers, more than twice the number expected. Leather lovers, girl jocks, cowboys, teens, white-haired dykes, P-Flaggers, gay and lesbian parents and their kids, people in all stages of transition, people in Gucci and people in absolute rags, and everyone in between.

In the magic of Miriam's lights, the crowd animated the Center—eating, drinking, cruising, buying T-shirts, writing checks, pledging money, and celebrating Sandy's life. With the main program scheduled to begin at eight, Allie hung out with Christina and Kyle at the stage. Usually a mountain of calm,

Allie was absolutely crazed, looking at her watch every five seconds. Joe and the sound crew were running very late. By eight-thirty, a sizeable crowd had gathered around the stage, waiting impatiently. It was now eight-thirty-one and counting.

Adjusting his earphones, Joe stood at the mixer, communicating with the tech on-stage. Something was way off with the main mic. Even after the tech counted from one to five a hundred times, nothing worked.

"What in *hell* is he doing up there?" Allie complained. "I thought they did the sound check..."

She was interrupted by a blast of static from the two huge speakers. Then, suddenly, everything worked! Allie made a quick call and heaved a sigh of relief. Instantly, a drumbeat began in the street out front—first one, then several, then many drums in unison—coming closer, until they actually vibrated the ground near the stage. Everyone lingering inside the Center flew out to see if an earthquake was happening.

A drumming group of eight women, including Nandi, with congas slung over their shoulders, made their way down 4th Avenue. Marcia and Garrett from the youth group came next, carrying a rainbow banner that said *Sandy Kramer Memorial Party*. Mentors, including Kevin and Angie, and more than forty teens followed the banner and the compelling drumbeat. From the street through the parking lot, the crowd parted to let the procession through and onto the stage.

When the drums stopped, there was a profound silence, then *HUGE* applause. Kevin and the two teens carrying the banner installed it across the back of the stage. There was more applause, and still more as the drummers left the stage. The youth, Kevin, and Angie remained onstage, looking out at the crowd in amazement. Angie winked at Kyle. Allie pulled herself together. Her eyes were filled with tears.

Marcia, Sandy's girlfriend, and Garrett stepped up to the mics. Surprisingly poised, Marcia said, "Wow! This is awesome. On behalf of the Tucson LGBTQ Youth Group, welcome to the Sandy Kramer Annual Memorial Bash!"

Allie looked at Christina, "*Annual?*"

Her lover whispered, "She's just like you, Al."

Garrett said, "Five years ago, the youth group was Allie and Kevin and four teens. Now we have over sixty kids and four mentors. Tonight we have a lot more. We have all of you. Thanks for coming!"

There was wild applause.

Marcia waited for the roar to die down, and then said, "Let's take a moment of silence for Sandy—and for a better world. Free from prejudice. And filled with justice and love. We love you, Sandy."

There was a murmur of assent, then a moment of silence.

Afterward, Marcia continued, "Thanks. Now, please join me in a moment of silence for Sandy's parents."

Kyle and Allie shot each other a look of surprise. There was minor grumbling, then a profound silence that carried a healing wave of forgiveness through the crowd.

Marcia wrapped up, "Alright! And now we formally dedicate this night to our friend, Sandy Kramer. I know she's here."

They both happily added, "Have a blast, everyone!"

The crowd cheered again.

Garrett said, "And now we'd like to introduce Allie...Jones!"

Surprised by all the applause for her, Allie stepped onto the stage and took the mic. She started quietly, "Sandy was a brilliant, beautiful kid. She struggled to be herself—like a wildflower trying to grow in asphalt. Sandy didn't make it. But, thankfully, all of us here have made it to this place, this night, to celebrate her life." She continued, louder, "AND WE KNOW HOW TO CELEBRATE!"

Voices from the crowd yelled, "YEAH!"

"So, we're gonna party. And we're gonna make a difference!" Allie continued, "We're gonna give something back. Like tons of money to this youth group. Or make a pledge. Or give our time." She pointed to the group on the stage, "Here they are—strong and beautiful and proud. Let's put our hands together for our awesome youth group!"

When the applause died down, Allie continued more quietly yet with more determination. "When most of us were teens, we endured prejudice, bigotry and the trauma of being bullied or closeted. And when we finally grew up, we took our freedom and never looked back."

Someone in the audience yelled, "Hell, yeah!" and there was a ripple of laughter through the crowd.

Allie smiled and continued, "Well, now it's time to look back. You'll see teens like Sandy, and these beautiful kids in our group, coming up behind you. And too many of them are still going through the same hell. And this ABSOLUTELY has to stop..."

The crowd cheered and broke into applause.

Allie continued, "Right here. Right now. In Tucson, Arizona. Tonight."

There was louder applause.

"So look back, hold out your hands and your hearts, and grab onto all these beautiful queer kids coming up behind you. If you've already donated, heartfelt thanks! And now go back inside and pledge twice as much. You know you can afford it!

We're their family. Show them what we mean by love and pride and power and compassion. C'mon, everyone! It's time to change the world!"

The crowd went wild. Allie left the stage and DJ took over.

"Keep it up," DJ encouraged, putting her hands together. "Let's have a hand for the volunteers...Give it up for everyone who's already contributed. And everyone who's about to. And special thanks to Joe over there at the mixer. He and Music City made the first $5,000 donation...Yeah, let's hear it! Who's gonna match it? Come on—you can make a pledge any time tonight."

Kevin's partner Ed yelled, "I'll do it!" and Kevin ran off the stage and kissed him passionately in front of everyone. When the whistling and applause died down, DJ shouted out into the heavens, "Alright! This night's for you, Sandy. We love you, grrl!" Then to the crowd, "C'mon, everybody, let's party!"

And they did! The minute Theresa's salsa-rock band launched into their first cumbia, dancers crowded the parking lot. After Kevin made another impassioned pitch for the youth group, *Severe Tire Damage* laid down a harder, rock and rap set. At the next break, the moon rose up overhead. Angie made the final pitch as Kyle, Nandi, and their band set up. Inspired, they played an amazing mix of danceable tunes, including a couple of Kyle's originals. The backup singers joined them in two covers that everyone knew well.

Toward the end of their set, DJ spied Billie Knight in the audience and called her onto the stage. Reluctant, Billie hesitated at first, but the lesbians in the crowd began chanting, "Billie! Billie! Billie!"

Giving in, she bounded up the steps to the stage, whispered a minute with Kyle and Nandi, and then took the mic, "Here's a simple song about love, and there's a lot of it going around here tonight!"

Kyle started a keyboard intro. She and Nandi filled in with harmonies on the chorus, knowing the ballad by heart. The band fell in behind them on the second verse, and the backup singers joined in, too. Billie's classic was, all at once, nostalgic and new. Lovers slow danced. Others put their arms around their neighbors and sang along in front of the stage.

When Billie's song ended and the applause began, DJ took the mic and stepped in. "Let's hear it for Billie Knight! And our own backup singers and band!"

The crowd knew she was wrapping up and began yelling, "*More! More!*"

DJ continued, "What a night! Was that the best party EVER?"

The crowd screamed and whistled. Not giving up, some people yelled, "More!"

DJ pressed on, feeling the significance of the moment. "Thank you, beautiful family! We've raised over forty-six thousand dollars tonight, and still counting! Good job, people! Let's hit fifty before we go!"

Huge applause.

"This one really *is* our last song. Kyle wrote it for Sandy and for all of us here tonight. THANK YOU, EVERYONE. THANK YOU FOR COMING! *Goodnight!*"

The crowd cheered, then quieted as Kyle began the introduction. The slow, gospel piano magnetized the crowd toward the stage, into silence, and closer to each other. When Nandi began her magic, *everyone* joined hands or put their arms around each other. After Kyle's spare harmony on the first chorus, and the backups' stellar performance on the second, Billie joined Nandi at her mic. Nandi gestured for members of the other bands to join them on-stage, too. Each verse built in intensity. By the last chorus, most of the crowd was singing in harmony, too.

Goodnight

When the night fills with fear
　　Reach for me. I'll be here
When the stars shine above
Feel the light. Feel the love

And we'll all go together
Like a shepherd with his sheep
'Tho the night is dark and deep
And we'll all be together. C'mon, and hold out your hand
And we'll all see the sun risin' over this land
Goodnight. Goodnight
Baby, goodnight. Goodnight

And we'll all go together
Like a shepherdess with her sheep
'Tho the way is hard and steep
And we'll all be together. And we'll all lend a hand
And we'll all see the sun shinin' over this land
Goodnight. Goodnight
Baby, goodnight. Goodnight

When the song ended, DJ said tenderly into the mic, "Be well, everyone. See you next year!"

Fulfilled, the crowd slowly disbursed. By eleven-thirty, the street was almost empty, fulfilling Allie's promise to the neighbors and the police. By midnight, it was just a handful of teens and volunteers cleaning up the Center and the parking lot. Kyle and Nandi stashed their gear in Kyle's truck, and Nandi headed for the bar with women from their band and Theresa's. Kyle and DJ stayed on to help Joe pack up. Around one, Joe and the techs pulled out in the Music City truck, and DJ left for the bar.

Kyle went to find Angie inside the Center and pulled her into a kiss. They melted into each other in a natural, easy way.

"Amazing night, wasn't it?"

"Incredible. Your song is still in my head."

"Ready to go?" Angie's closeness was giving Kyle wonderful ideas about how to end the night.

"I'm just gonna take Marcia home first. Allie's got everybody else. Come with me?"

Kyle flinched only slightly about Angie's detour. It was obvious that tonight, of all nights, Sandy's girlfriend needed Angie's support. So, she smiled and replied, "Yes, I'll come—but later, home in bed, making love."

Angie smiled seductively, "I can arrange that." She kissed Kyle tenderly. "No worries. I'll be home soon."

By two-thirty, both Kyle and Nandi were fast asleep. Even Rat did not stir as Angie slipped into bed next to Kyle, exhausted.

- 41 -

Sunday noon after the benefit, Kyle's truck screeched into a parking space in front of the Greenery, late for brunch with the pals. Several motorcycle dykes putting on their helmets startled at their noisy arrival. When they recognized Kyle and Nandi from Sandy's concert, they came right over.

"You guys were awesome last night!" said a big woman, impressive in leather. "You got a CD?"

Nandi replied, "Not yet. Maybe soon."

"You got any more gigs coming up?"

"Maybe next year's party. We're from San Diego," said Nandi. "Going home in a couple days."

"Three days!" interrupted Kyle. Everyone looked her way. Embarrassed, she added, "Jeez, it *is* only two days. Anyway, thanks a lot, guys."

Kyle and Angie went into the Greenery while Nandi stayed behind to talk with the band's admirers. Nandi's whole experience of Tucson centered around the band and the benefit, and it galvanized her focus on their music, especially now that Kyle was writing again. For Nandi, it meant re-organizing the band and recording a demo CD in San Diego. Hopefully, they could then book weekend and holiday gigs in Tucson and southern California.

"My name's Nandi Johnson. Let's keep in touch on Facebook. We want to sell a CD online..."

Excited, the biker interjected, "How about a CD release party in Tucson?"

"Awesome idea!" exclaimed Nandi.

Another biker added, "We'd come for sure!"

Meanwhile, at the pals' table, Kyle gave everyone a quick hug and then slumped down into a chair next to Allie. DJ and Allie exchanged worried looks. Angie hugged everyone and then sat across from Kyle. She gave Allie a look that said *help!* Allie nodded.

Oblivious to the happy group around her, Kyle chose to scan the Greenery crowd instead. She noticed Billie Knight and the owner having their own private breakfast in a remote corner. Her heart warmed. They seemed wonderfully close, leaning in toward each other and rapt in a great conversation. No one disturbed them. She envied them immensely. *Why aren't Angie and I alone right now? I can't believe she cares about me—but she does! She's taking off work tomorrow to be with me. Maybe someday I'll be like Billie, visiting my lover in Tucson. Maybe that's the way to keep a long distance relationship long!*

When Nandi arrived at the table, the group turned to her with a blast of congratulations, standing up to hug her and sing her praises.

That gave DJ the chance to ask, "Okay, Kyle. What's up? A hangover? No sleep?"

Kyle was in no mood. "It's hard to leave, that's all. I'm gonna miss Angie. And you guys, too, if I'm leaving on Tuesday."

DJ put her hand to her forehead dramatically. "You'll miss *her*. I'll miss *you*..."

Allie knew that Kyle was serious. "What do you mean *if* you're leaving?"

Kyle deflected, unaware that she had said *if*. "I mean next week at this time, I'll be four hundred miles away. It might as well be a million..."

Nandi said, "You've been a million miles away all morning..."

Kyle could only laugh, and that allowed everyone else to laugh, too.

Over iced mochas and breakfast, the group told hilarious and touching stories about their experiences at the benefit. Nandi shared the conversation she'd just had with the bikers, and the pals got excited about the band's encore at next year's event. Allie was blown away that it would become an annual fundraiser and a legacy for Sandy. DJ remembered how Marcia called a moment of silence for Sandy's parents. Angie shared how the teens cried as they set up Sandy's room, and greeted everyone at the benefit with smiles and stories, even though their hearts were breaking.

Kyle shared how last night's performance was her best ever. She was grateful that Nandi came, and grateful for the musicians that volunteered for the band—they got really good, really fast. The drummer, especially, was amazing. It was thrilling to play her new song, *Goodnight*, to that beautiful crowd, under the stars and Miriam's lights, with Nandi and the band and the backups. And Billie Knight joining in! It was a night she would always remember...

They reminisced back to Sandy's memorial service and the hurried preparations that were so much work and so much fun. And nobody could believe they raised $50,000! And counting—with checks expected to come in for at least another week.

Later, as they lingered over goodbyes, Kyle quietly asked Allie for advice.

"Al, did you ever decide to change your life because of your lover?"

"On a daily basis."

Kyle laughed. "C'mon, Al. I mean a big thing. Like where you live. That changes everything—your job, your friends, you know...everything."

"Like I said, on a daily basis."

They both laughed.

Allie added, "Changing where you live doesn't mean you give up your life. The place has to work for both of you. But, now your lives can...touch...every day."

"Well, I got that part right!"

Allie nodded toward Angie. "Talk to her, Kyle. Really talk. Just spend time with her 'til you go. We'll take care of Nandi."

"Thanks, Al. You're the best."

"Good luck, Kyle. I think you really care about her."

"Yeah." Kyle had opened up as much as she could, much more than she'd planned. It was a little scary that Allie already knew her so well, after just two months.

"Will I see you before you go?"

"Yeah," smiled Kyle, giving Allie an especially warm hug in case it wasn't true.

On her way out, Kyle followed an impulse to thank Billie for last night. She hesitated to interrupt her, but she *had* to honor Billie's generosity, in case she never had another chance. Billie and Kathryn, the Greenery's owner, turned and smiled as she entered their space.

Kyle felt welcome and relieved. "I don't want to disturb you, but thanks, Billie, for last night. It was the honor of a lifetime to sing with you!"

Billie replied, "*Goodnight* is a super song, Kyle. I'd love to make it the last song on my new album. I'm leaving for the airport in ten minutes, so could you call me?"

Shocked, Kyle said, "What? Uh...yeah. Yes! Absolutely."

"Got your phone? I'll give you my cell number."

Billie gave Kyle the number, then got up and hugged her goodbye. It was a warm hug between friends, not an obligatory one. Surprised at herself, Kyle hugged Billie back with a monstrous flow of love rising in her chest. Then, she smiled and nodded to Kathryn, and left without another word.

It would take her days to replay this moment in her mind a million times and get over the shock.

- 42 -

After brunch, Angie went to the Center with Allie for a victory debriefing with the youth group. Kyle went home to pack, which is always hell, even if you want to go where you're going. Nandi went out with the pals.

Some time after three, Kyle's truck pulled up in front of Angie's house. She never had enough time these days. She looked at her watch. Three twenty. *Shit!* She was stupidly late, but incredibly eager to pick up Angie and retreat into their own world. She was excited to tell her about Billie Knight. She hadn't told anyone yet and wanted Angie to be the first.

Kyle bounded up the front steps and rang the doorbell. Standing there waiting, she cringed momentarily, remembering their horrendous first date after Mexico. Then, she laughed out loud. It had all been totally worth it. She rang the doorbell again, harder, listening to make sure it was working. It was. She tried the door. It was locked. She rang the bell again, and then went around to the back. Locked. No cars. Angie's car was still at Kyle's from last night. No Miriam or Daniela...

Annoyed, Kyle checked her phone and found Angie's *sorry running late* text. She couldn't believe it. *Where is she?* Kyle's happy excitement turned to hurt, and a seed of anger began growing in her mind. She went back to the front steps, sat down in the blazing August sun, and grew unbearably hot within minutes. Next door, a middle-aged neighbor in plaid shorts and brown socks was weed-whacking, with a horrible effect on Kyle's nerves. As soon as there was a moment of silence, the infernal noise buzzed up again full blast. The guy's t-shirt, soaked through with sweat, clung to his paunchy stomach. Bits of flung grass stuck to his hairy legs. Sweat beaded up on his forehead and poured down his face. Sweat was starting to soak through Kyle's shirt, too. She was feeling a little nauseous.

Seeking relief from the sun and the racket, Kyle went back to lean against her truck, which she'd parked under a scrawny mesquite tree. Even the metal on the truck was hot. A nasty headache was mushrooming into her awareness, along with rapidly growing anger. *She doesn't care about me. She's already written me off. Why am I stupid enough to wait for her?*

The weed-whacking continued randomly off and on while Kyle silently ranted about Angie being late. Severely overheated, the sharp pain behind her eyes gradually overtook even those angry thoughts. After ten minutes that felt like ninety, Kevin's car pulled up.

Leaping out, Angie said, "Kyle, I'm sorry. Come in with me. I just have to get my stuff." She grabbed Kyle's hand and pulled her happily up the front steps.

As Angie unlocked the door, Kyle met her gaze with cold eyes. "You're *sorry*."

"YES, I'm really really sorry!" Angie was worried about Kyle's flushed face and sweat-soaked shirt. Flinging the door open, she said, "Come in and get some water..."

Irrationally, Kyle stood her ground outside. She blurted out, "How could you be this late with only thirty-six hours left?"

Angie's mouth involuntarily leaked a smile, happy that Kyle was counting the hours, too.

Thinking that Angie was laughing at her, Kyle added resentfully, "And you don't give a shit." The weed-whacker buzzed on, briefly, and Kyle spoke louder, "You think this is funny."

"Kyle, why would you *say* that? Come in!"

Quiet reigned again as the neighbor began to rake up cuttings nearby. Kyle imagined he could now overhear every word. She felt embarrassed and somehow exposed.

"I sat here like an idiot. I was so excited to take you home and finally be alone..."

Angie replied, "Kyle, I'm excited, too. Come *in*. I've *got* to get you some water..." Angie disappeared into the house, leaving the door open.

Kyle looked into the empty doorway, seeing only the reflection of her own emptiness. She felt sick and abandoned. Her head was about to explode. Her heart was racing. *I can't do this now!* With a terrible cacophony of sadness, anger, and pain pounding in her head and her chest, Kyle turned and fled down the stairs, leaving everything she wanted behind.

J. Anderson

When Angie heard Kyle's engine turn over, she ran through the living room to the door, spilling ice water everywhere. Empty glass in hand, she stood there incredulous as the truck left rubber and sped away without her.

- 43 -

Ten minutes after she left Angie's, Kyle texted her from the bar: "Not feeling well. Need to be alone for just an hour or two. Will come back. Sorry!"

Completely at a loss, Angie texted: *OK. Feel better. Drink water! Call me.*

Putting down her phone, she made a silent promise to wait for Kyle to extricate herself from her current black hole. She wouldn't pressure her or try to help. She would just wait. With only today and tomorrow left to be together, it would be hard, but not the end of the world.

Some time later, Kyle leaned on her elbow at the bar, wasted. She had started with a big glass of water, but then took full advantage of happy hour. Everyone who'd heard her band at Sandy's party wanted to buy her a drink and, of course, she let them. Fortunately, the heat-induced headache was down to a three from its original ten and, now, she could take time to think things through. She still felt bent about Angie, although by now she had pretty much forgotten why she got so insanely mad. She yearned to be with her, to make love, and forget about the future—and the past. Like it or not, this was a defining moment for them, and she had nothing to offer except, obviously, an apology.

She had no idea what time it was. To be safe, she texted Angie: *Still chilling—literally. Feeling better. Sorry!*

Angie texted: *Are you okay? Should I come over?*

Kyle replied: *No. I'll get you soon. I'll call when I leave.*

Kyle ordered one last drink for courage, a double shot. The bartender brought a double latte instead, laughing off Kyle's protest. She'd be damned if she'd drink it. Besides, she could take a cab home, if necessary, when she was good and ready. And if she were ready, she would already be home now, thank you very much.

Kyle kept trying to order what she promised would be her last drink, but the bartender ignored her. Even without knowing about Kyle's run-in with the sun, the bartender could see that she didn't need another drop of alcohol. Kyle was too stubborn to surrender and leave. She stared into her empty glass and drank the ice as it melted.

She texted Angie: *I'll be there in an hour.*

Without being asked, the bartender refilled her glass of water—twice. Kyle downed it obediently, sucking up and acting sober, at least in her own mind. After another ten minutes of badgering, the bartender reluctantly delivered Kyle's double shot of vodka and Rose's lime juice, considerably watered down. Nevertheless, it immediately boosted Kyle's headache, turned her stomach, and decimated her clarity and coordination.

Gesturing to the bartender, she yelled, "Hey, can you tone down those fucking lights in the mirror? I am respectly requencing...request-ening." She let it go at that.

The bartender called DJ and begged her to come to work early and take Kyle home. When DJ showed up around seven, Kyle bid everyone at the bar a theatrical goodnight, and DJ half guided and half dragged her to the car. That was the last thing Kyle could remember.

She awoke before dawn the next morning in her own bed, with all her clothes on, alone. Barely in time, she ran to the bathroom to vomit. At some point, she must have been sick in the middle of the night because the toilet seat was still up.

She groaned involuntarily as yesterday's altercation on Angie's porch came back to her. *We were both late. Why in hell did I leave? We could have fought about it and had great make-up sex. We'd be together now. I'm such an idiot!*

Despite deep regrets, the headache, and the all-pervasive, grey mood that accompanies a hangover, she checked her phone for messages. There was only one message—an excruciatingly long one from DJ explaining how she got home last night. DJ said she called Angie right away, so she wouldn't worry about Kyle.

Oh, god, no!

No messages from Angie since yesterday afternoon.

Kyle grimaced. She had squandered their precious time. Exactly what she accused Angie of doing. At least there was today, and she vowed not to ruin it! She had to call Angie. But, it was not quite five a.m.

She silently made her way to the kitchen, determined not to wake Nandi and trigger an unwanted conversation. As always, Rat came to rub against her legs as she made coffee. Kyle drank it slowly, petting Rat in her lap. Although she despised herself, Rat purred contentedly and loved her anyway.

A shower helped tremendously.

Afterward, Kyle threw a bottle of water into her backpack. She had to go somewhere else to pull herself together. She left Nandi a brief note and headed for Sabino Canyon to escape and maybe find a little clarity and peace before going to Angie's.

She arrived just after dawn. Zealous runners and hikers were already doing their thing. Kyle took a well-worn trail along the winding stream into the canyon. The early morning was exquisite: the coolness, the breeze, the cactus and wildflowers, the big sky, the simple constant of the rippling stream, and the big trees lining the banks. Her body felt good, moving easily along the trail. The stream seemed to come along with her, or she with the stream. She knew her life had to move, too—to decide something, do something!

Angie is waiting for me. That makes me insanely lucky! She's been fearless and I've been...chickenshit! I want her. I know it. I have to give it a chance, whatever happens. Maybe I can take Nandi home tomorrow, and then come back for a few days before U of A starts. Maybe even drive back here with Liz and then fly home. Yes—that's it! That will show her I want more than just a hot summer affair...

Feeling hopeful, Kyle stopped for a drink of water. She lay down to rest momentarily on a flat rock shaded by cottonwoods at the edge of the water. Listening to the rippling of the stream and the wind in the trees, she watched the clouds cross the blue sky through the shimmering leaves. When she closed her eyes, she fell deeply asleep.

She awoke to the noise of little kids screaming and laughing. She sat up slowly. Groggy and warm, she was now in sunlight, like a lizard on a rock. Shielding her eyes, she could make out four or five kids cannonballing into the water off a rock ledge just upstream. Their happy, high-pitched voices pierced the last of her headache, yet made her smile. Two women read their books nearby, under the shade of a big cottonwood, occasionally looking up to check their kids.

Kyle found her pack and took a long drink of water. Sore from an hour and a half on her bed of rock, she took off her hiking boots and waded into the stream up to her knees. It felt amazingly good to splash her face and neck with cold, cold water, the runoff from the Catalina mountains. The kids finally noticed her in the water. Except for the littlest girl, they paid no attention.

"Hey!" she called to Kyle in a loud, tiny voice. She was about six, swimming in just her underpants.

"Hey!" said Kyle. One of the women looked up, decided Kyle was okay, and returned to her book. She knew what was coming.

"Watch me jump," demanded the little girl, jumping straight into the water, feet first.

Kyle yelled, "Awesome."

"I can do a cannonball." She ran back and waited her turn to mount the big rock. "Watch!" she yelled to Kyle, then jumped.

"Wanna do one?" She smiled ecstatically as she wiped the water from her eyes and splashed over to Kyle.

"Uh, maybe next time," Kyle hesitated. "I don't have my bathing suit."

That meant nothing to the girl. She offered Kyle her hand, "Come *on!*"

Kyle stripped to her undershirt, threw her shirt on the bank, and emptied her pockets. She let the little girl take her to the rock ledge. One boy ran ahead to get his turn in. The other kids made way for them.

"Watch me first," commanded the little girl, taking off for her absolutely best jump yet. Then, from the water, she said, "Okay, now you do it."

"How deep is it?" asked Kyle.

The boy in the water, said, "This high." It was almost up to his shoulders.

Good. She wouldn't break a leg. She cannonballed into the water. The shock was exhilarating. She somersaulted, and then opened her eyes to the blue sky and a horizon full of cottonwoods and cactus. Kids clapping at the somersault. Mothers smiling at her from their books. Cold, cold water. She felt absolutely, wonderfully alive. Treading water for a moment, she took in the simple magic of the world.

"Come *on!*" called the little girl, already waiting her turn in line. "What are you doing out there?"

Oh my god! What AM I doing out here?

In a flash, she was out of the water, checking her phone. Angie had called her. She started to call back, but stopped. Grabbing her stuff, she bounded down the trail, her wet clothes cooling her. She absolutely had to talk with Angie in person, touching, looking into her eyes, sensing her feelings.

At the truck, she texted: *On my way...*

She took off maniacally in the truck, and then consciously slowed down. It would be too ridiculous to die on the way to Angie's. Her phone rang. Nandi. She ignored it.

Twenty minutes later, she found herself ringing Angie's doorbell without a plan or coherent thought in her head, just a flood of emotion.

Angie opened the door. "Kyle!" A look flashed across her face like she had seen an angel. Likely, Kyle was too self-absorbed to notice.

"Can I come in? I always fuck up out here."

They both laughed as Kyle stepped into the living room and stopped.

"Are you okay?"

Realizing her clothes were still wet, Kyle said, "I can't sit down. I'm still wet from uh, swimming."

"God, I'm glad you're here. Are you alright?"

"Yeah. Actually, I'm...finally...good! You look amazing!" She had to kiss Angie, and felt the thrill and rightness of it as they melted together. But, soon she pulled away, before the clarity of that moment in the stream faded away. "Listen, I…uh...Jesus, this is hard. I'm sorry I freaked out yesterday. It hurt...my feelings...that you weren't there...for me." She closed her eyes for a moment, trying to form a coherent thought. "You can really hurt me now, Ange—if I let you. And I'm scared."

Angie had the good sense just to listen.

Kyle continued, "I mean, you and I were both supposed to leave after the summer, right? It was supposed to be *light*." Her eyes filled with tears. "Well it isn't. Is it?"

"No."

"Suddenly *you're* gonna stay in Tucson. And I have to react…"

"Kyle, you're one of the reasons I'm staying. I knew a San Diego-New York thing would never work."

"But now it's all on me. Can't you see that? What happens to us. And you're not helping, believe me."

"What do you mean? I'm *staying*..."

Kyle argued, "Of course you're staying. Your whole life is here...But, you never asked *me* to stay in Tucson. How am I supposed to know what you want?"

"Well, I'll tell you now. I want you to stay." Angie bravely added, "I want you...close to me."

Kyle stepped closer to Angie and searched her eyes.

Angie continued, "But, it can't be only what I want. You've got to decide, just like you told me. What do *you* wanna do?"

Kyle said, "Run like hell and never look back."

They laughed. Somehow the naked truth seemed much less threatening than the weeks of silence had been.

Kyle confessed, "But if I run, it's the end of the story. We need more time, Ange. To give us a chance..."

Angie's eyes filled with tears. "Kyle..."

"I want to stay in Tucson with you, Ange. Uh—I mean I'll stay with Liz. Or get a place of my own." Kyle kept on, while her courage lasted. "Can we just see what happens?" She took a breath. "I...I think I love you, Ange." She sighed, then said more courageously, "I love you. I know I do."

"I love you, too, Kyle," Angie said, simply. She put her arms around Kyle, embracing her wet clothes. "I've been waiting for you for a long, long time."

- 44 -

Day of departure! DJ and Angie sat on Kyle's dining room floor, painting a huge *WELCOME HOME LIZ* banner. Taking frequent breaks from cleaning up the house, Kyle kissed Angie and joked with DJ. She was high as a kite.

In the guest bedroom, Nandi packed the last of her things, avoiding the others. She found Kyle almost unbearable. She couldn't believe Kyle was going to take her to San Diego, clear out the guest house, turn around, and come back in a few days! Yesterday, Kyle had asked her to come live in Tucson, too—talking about the music and Allie and the pals, and she would pay the rent 'til Nandi got a job. Out of her fuckin' mind in love.

But, Nandi was all set to move back into her room at Kay's.

She had come here on a two week leave of absence from work. She had to return tomorrow or risk getting fired. Kyle might have a life here, but hers was in San Diego, even without Jackie. But, now, life would be doubly lonely without Kyle.

Kyle moved her suitcase and music gear into the guest bedroom while Nandi finished packing.

"Girlfriend?" Kyle finally broke the painful silence between them.

"Yeah?"

"Why won't you come back here with me?"

"It's your gig, Kyle."

"It's our time to do the music. What about Billie? Isn't that a sign? I mean, it's more than a sign!"

"Yeah, well..."

"C'mon, I mean a song for Billie's album—that's huge! If you're here, we can do the CD and everything. Wasn't it amazing to sing together again? They love us here!"

"They love *you* here."

"C'mon. You need to be here. Give it a shot for six months."

"It's your gig..."

"It's our gig."

"I mean Angie."

"What about Angie? We're not gonna live together yet. I'm not that stupid! *We* should get a place, you and me! C'mon, six months...see if you like it."

"I don't get it. Liz said you can stay here..."

"Goddammit, Nan. That's not the point. I want us to go for it. I want us to do a CD or YouTube or *something*. I want you to get your friggin' stuff and come back with me, for God's sake!"

Lovers

"You really mean it, don't you?"

"What do I have to do? Tattoo it on my forehead?"

Nandi laughed, "DJ is rubbing off on you."

They hadn't heard Angie and DJ greet Allie as she came to say a quick goodbye on her lunch break. Now, they all burst into the bedroom.

"Kyle! You're coming back! Alright!" said Allie, giving her a big hug. "Nandi, what about you?"

Nandi was touched that Allie asked about her, but said, "What do you mean?"

Without thinking, Allie took Nandi's hands and said, "You've gotta come back. Don't you feel it?"

Nandi said nothing, but Allie's eyes held her.

"You need to sing the songs she's gonna write. She needs to write the songs you're gonna sing. And the pals love you already. How great is this gonna be?"

"Nobody else ever let me sing backup," confessed DJ, standing in the doorway.

"You've gotta stay," said Angie.

Kyle watched Nandi responding, opening up. She met Kyle's eyes with a question.

Kyle looked back with love and resolve. "I'm getting your stuff outa the truck right now."

"Okay," said Nandi, tentatively.

"*WHAT?* You're gonna do it?" Kyle couldn't believe her ears.

"Yeah, we're gonna do it," grinned Nandi, starting off the silly rapper handshake they did after every performance.

Allie offered, "Chris and I can take Michelle for a few days."

"She'd better come with us," said Nandi. "She's not

as...polite...as she looks!"

They all laughed. In no stretch of the imagination had any of them thought of Michelle as well-behaved.

"I've got Rat covered," said Angie, already a big fan.

"This is so cool!" DJ sniffed, with tears beginning to run down her cheeks.

Allie dug the bandanna out of her back pocket for DJ.

DJ blew her nose. "This is so ridiculous," she protested. "Why am I crying?"

DEDICATION

I'll cut to the chase. If you liked *LOVERS* and are inspired by Kyle, Angie, and their friends' support of LGBTQ youth, please join them—in real life—by donating to the brand new *Thornhill-Lopez Center on 4th* at http://saaf.org/ways-to-support/center-on-4th/

Years ago when I wrote *LOVERS*, Tucson's LGBTQ youth program was housed in a small, 1-room storefront on 4th Avenue. So, my imagination created a much bigger and better Center. Novels are fiction, so hey! While preparing to publish the book, I learned that a new, 5,000 square foot *Center on 4th* will open this winter. It's definitely a dream come true!

The Center on 4th will include a big events space, meeting rooms, computer center, offices, industrial kitchen, and an open air patio—a much needed oasis for our LGBTQ youth! There's even a parking lot for a benefit concert like Kyle and Nandi's. Ongoing programs will include:

- Adult support and referrals
- Peer support—a welcoming space to hang out
- Sex positive education
- HIV prevention, testing, and counseling
- Suicide, violence, and substance abuse prevention
- Life skills, advocacy, and youth-led projects

- Support for homeless youth (40% of whom are LGBTQ), including food, clothing, showers, and housing assistance.

I'm proud to be a donor to *The Center on 4th* and happy to give 50% of the net proceeds from *LOVERS* to the Center. Today, with politicians making prejudice great again, the need for an LGBTQ youth Center is greater than ever. Many queer youth are living in fear of discrimination, exclusion, and/or bullying on a daily basis. Many face prejudice at home, in their schools, and in their churches—at the time when they are most emotionally vulnerable. *The Center on 4th* will be a welcoming, safe place for queer teens of all races, colors, religions, and abilities. The family that supports them can be us.

Please donate online or send a check (write *for Center on 4th* on the memo line) to:

The Center on 4th
c/o Southern Arizona AIDS Foundation
375 S. Euclid Ave.
Tucson, AZ 85719

Or, give to the LGBTQ youth programs in your city.

Thanks! This book is dedicated to you.

ABOUT THE AUTHOR

*L*OVERS is my first novel. Probably, it's like a dream where every character expresses a unique part of the dreamer. So, if you've read the book, you already know a lot about me! Not to mention the story arc, which sets up Kyle, Angie, and their friends to realize my own hopes and dreams. I'm grateful for the opportunity to write their story and a few of their songs, and I have a good feeling about their future!

Meanwhile, I'm part-time CEO of a small, local foundation devoted to youth voice and empowerment. I also practice and teach Reiki and meditation and hang out with a likable bunch of family and friends.

Thank you for reading *LOVERS!*